ESCAPE 2 EARTH

ESCAPE 2 EARTH

Lawrence Johnson Sr.

iUniverse, Inc.

New York Lincoln Shanghai

Escape 2 Earth

iUniverse books may be ordered through booksellers or by contacting:

iUniverse
2021 Pine Lake Road, Suite 100
Lincoln, NE 68512
www.iuniverse.com
1-800-Authors (1-800-288-4677)

ISBN-13: 978-0-595-38935-3 (pbk)
ISBN-13: 978-0-595-83318-4 (ebk)
ISBN-10: 0-595-38935-X (pbk)
ISBN-10: 0-595-83318-7 (ebk)

Printed in the United States of America

I am dedicating this book to the people that I love the most. Starting with my wife and friend Renea who has been the center of my universe for three decades. Thank you for all of your support. To my children Lawrence Jr. and Alicia who mean the world to me.

This project has become a reality because of the shinning star of this undertaking my daughter Lauren. She was typist, editor, critic, consultant, and my right arm. Thank you. I love you all.

Lawrence Johnson

FOREWORD

Alien warnings embedded in our crop circles have gone unnoticed, until now. Governments around the globe race against time to evacuate billions of inhabitants from the planet due to the discovery that Earth will be **destroyed in the year 2012, a mere eight years away.**

Where would we go? How would we get there? Who would be left behind? And why is one race of aliens plotting to keep us here?
These are just a few of the questions and obstacles faced on this **galactic odyssey by our trio of heroes** in Escape 2 Earth. Matt, Will, and Art are reluctantly drawn into an adventure by a **secret alien organization** that will unlock the mysteries of **Stonehenge, the White Pyramid of China, the Mayan calendar, and the Great Sphinx** in a scramble to help save the human race.

This epic quest for Earth's survival takes you from the powdery pink morning skies on the planet Lazon to the subterranean cities under planet Vada and the Whistling forest.

The battle between good and evil that began long ago in a far off galaxy is now being played out with the **survival of mankind at stake**. This sci-fi story is laced with a touch of **telepathy, deception, and a murder or two**. Discover the **hidden alien base** deep in the dark murky depths of the **Marianas Trench**, watch as the aliens prepare to celebrate at the **Festival of Life**. Who will survive the race to escape this **doomed planet**? It is anybody's guess. Who will Escape to Earth?

CHAPTER 1

▼

SIGNS OF LIFE

Matt watched quietly as the shadow of the helicopter danced along the backdrop of the fields below. The gentle August breeze swayed the golden carpet of wheat back and forth as the chopper passed overhead. Will sat just a few feet away from Matt but was totally oblivious to the scenery outside the window. Will is an oldies fanatic, to be more accurate a Motown Oldies fanatic. His collection of records and CD's would make Berry Gordy jealous. If you listen closely, you could hear the faint sounds of The Supremes singing "Baby Love" through Will's headphones as he sat with his head back, and eyes closed just taking in the music.

Twenty minutes later right in the middle of Martha and the Vandellas "Heat Wave" Matt gave Will a nudge "It's show time." said Matt pointing at the enormous crop circle dead ahead. Will removed the headphones, adjusted his sunglasses and the two men sprang into action grabbing their cameras and starting to angle for position to get the best shots. It was obvious that the two were used to working together by the way they moved about the aircraft, passing each other lenses, rolls of film and various other pieces of photo equipment with hardly a word exchanged between them. After a few helicopter passes over the football field-sized crop circle Matt motioned for the pilot to land.

Will looked at Matt as they walked toward the massive circle and said, "You know it does not have to end today, you still have time to change your mind." Matt had decided to call it quits. It was a bittersweet ending to a six-year working relationship. Sweet because they had just signed another book deal with a major publishing company, the largest deal they have ever had. Bitter, because it would be their last.

"Come on Will, what's the big deal? It's not as if you need the cash. The money you made in the 90's from those tech stocks alone should hold you until you find a new partner, not to mention your half of the book money." Matt was not even close, Will's motivation was not the money but the adventure of travel and a chance to hang with his old Army buddy and best friend. "New partner!" Will snapped back. "I don't need a new partner there's nothing wrong with the one I got."

When they reached the crop circle, it was back to business. They were the first to arrive. The intricate patterns within the crop circle were in pristine condition. They spent hours taking pictures, notes, measurements and interviewing the owners of the farm. When they were satisfied with the information they had gathered they headed back to the airport and home.

Will was unusually quiet on the flight home. Matt attempted to broach the subject of retirement. "I need to spend more time at home with Sara", he said hoping to garner some sympathy from Will. "You know, settle down, have a few kids, and become a real family man. I have been promising her for years and you know we aren't getting any younger." Will sat in silence. "You're not the one who has to listen to the endless stories about her biological clock. Anyway, I have already accepted the position at America's Pulse Magazine. I start the first of the year when old man Nelson retires." Will shook his head from side to side and sniggered. "You will be bored to tears within a month and you know I am right." Matt decided to ignore Will's comment and continued. "Sara and I are going to take a long overdue vacation. I'm going to sip a couple dozen yellowbirds, eat some conch fritters, listen to some steel drum music and have lots of sex." He turned to Will and smiled. "One day you are going to get married and then you will finally understand." Will laughed aloud. "Not me brother", he said with a wave of the hand. He put on his headphones, lowered his seat back, and closed his eyes. End of conversation.

Autumn had given way to winter and the leaves had fallen from the trees. Matt and Sara returned from their vacation weeks ago, Matt and Will was just wrapping up a successful book signing tour. Sales of their latest Crop Circle book had exceeded the expectations of the publishing company and the pressure was on their agent to get the duo to shoot another book in the spring. Felix was not the kind of man to take no for an answer. He was a short stubby guy whose suits always looked as if he had slept in them. However, looks can be deceiving. Felix was as crafty as they come. He booked all three-book deals for Matt and Will, and he was gunning for number four. Felix invited them to the publishing companies' Christmas Party. Matt was reluctant but Felix badgered Matt until he agreed to show.

It was a very cold night in D.C and it had begun to snow. When Matt arrived at the party, Will was already there. He could tell by the look on Matt's face that he would rather be anywhere but there. "Come on Matt loosen up, this is supposed to be a party not a wake. Come on, let's get a couple of drinks and mingle." Matt decided not to be a party pooper now that he was there. Will ordered a scotch and Matt a Heineken. Practically, everyone there were writers or worked in publishing. No one there seemed interested in photographers or crop circles, no one except Arthur that is. Arthur sat alone looking out the window at the falling snow. "These seats taken?" Will asked. Arthur looked up from the rims of his glasses and said, "No, be my guest" "Hi, I'm Matt, and this is my buddy and business partner Will." "I am Arthur, Arthur Collins". He said as he extended his hand to shake Matt's hand. "Are you two writers?" "Afraid not" said Will. "We are just photographers. We did have a book published a few months ago though. How about you Arthur, you a writer?" "No, no" said Arthur shaking his head. "I am a computer tech and its Art, mostly everyone calls me Art except my mom." As the evening progressed and the conversation turned to the crop circles, Art became more and more fascinated with each story that Will and Matt told.

"So you guys haven't been able to decipher any of the symbols in all these years huh?" "No." said Will. "Not a one and neither have anyone else." Added Matt. Art scanned the room looking for eavesdroppers; he leaned forward and began to speak in a slow whisper. "I am part of a team building a new super computer over at CBT electronics. Actually, there are seven teams of five. We have been working day and night for the last ten months. I am the team leader for the uploading and testing unit of the project. We have only completed about forty-seven percent of the upload but if you two are willing, I would like to run your photographs through our computer and maybe we can be the first to come up with a break-through on this crop circle mystery. What do ya think?" Matt and Will stared at each other; they could not believe what they were hearing. For years, they have been baffled by the circles, and interpreting them has been an elusive goal up until now. Here was this man a total stranger offering them the chance of a lifetime. "Yeah, sure of course!" they both responded with enthusiasm. "When can we get started?" "Lower your voices", Arthur cautioned. "Are you tring to get me sacked?" "You must understand that this is all very unofficial. No one must know." Will and Matt had found an ally. They knew that by reading the crop circles that the puzzles would finally be solved and their long journey would finally come to an end. Little did they know that this was just the beginning of an unbelievable discovery that would not only change their lives but the lives that every living soul on the planet.

CHAPTER 2

▼

REVELATIONS

New Year's Eve seemed to come a bit faster this year. As in years past Sara and Matt invited about twenty of their closest friends and relatives over to party, and ring in the New Year. "Come on in Art, glad you could make it". Matt shook his hand and took his coat. "Help yourself to the food over there and grab yourself a glass of champagne, I am about to make a very special announcement." As Art made his way through the crowded room, he spotted Will waving frantically trying to get his attention. "Hey, Will how's it going? Happy New Year!" "Happy New Year to you too Art. Any news yet on the you know what?" "No", Art replied, "I still need a few more days to add more data and do a bit of tweaking."

Just then, Matt stood atop a dinning room chair and clanged a spoon against his glass. *Clang, clang, clang.* "May I have everyone's attention please?" Someone turned down the music as Sara's sister weaved her way through the crowed room filling everyone's glass with champagne. "This year has brought many new changes in my life, but none more exciting or important than hearing the news that I will soon become a father. Yes, Sara and I are having a baby." The partygoers erupted into cheers and applause. "I would like to toast my lovely wife Sara and to the soon to be new addition to our family." When Matt stepped down from the chair, Will whispered in his ear. "Must have been all of those conch fritters Sara fed you on vacation." "I heard that Will, Sara said with a smile. Will took Matt's place on the chair. "Raise your glasses high and toast with me to the finest most deserving couple that I have ever had the privilege to call my friends.

May all of your children be healthy, happy, and wise." Once again, the crowd raised their glasses and joined Will in toasting the expectant couple.

After the party, Will stayed behind to help clean up. He was collecting cups in the front room when Sara called him into the kitchen. "Hey Will, put that stuff down. Matt and I want to talk to you." Will put down the trash and headed for the kitchen. "I am not so good at changing diapers" he joked. "Pull up a chair. Matt and I want to ask you something." Before Will's butt could hit the seat, Matt just blurted it out. "Sara and I would like for you to be our baby's God Father. I know it is early and Sara's grandmother thinks that it is bad luck to name God Parents before the baby is born but that's just an old wives' tale. You were the Best Man at our wedding and our first and only choice for God Father. You don't have to give us your answer right now; we don't want to rush..." but before Matt could finish Will stood up, bowed slightly, and said, "I would con- sider it a privilege and an honor to be the God Father to your first born." It was clear to Sara and Matt that Will was deeply moved by their offer.

A few days later, at the crack of dawn, Will was jolted from his sleep by the ringing of the phone on his nightstand. He was not a happy camper, especially at this time of the morning. Gayle stayed over last night and Will had only slept for a few hours. "This had better be good", he mumbled into the receiver. "Top of the morning mate. It's Art." His British accent was a dead giveaway. "I knew how eager you were to hear the results of our little test so I rang you straightaway." Will propped himself up on one shoulder and said "Yeah, well don't keep me hanging." "Well" said Art "We came up dry, empty" "Empty!" barked Will. "You mean we got nothing?" "That's right nada, so far, but don't be discouraged we still have almost 18% more to upload into the system some very important stuff like languages, landmarks, solar systems. I have to follow the order that is passed down to me by the suits upstairs or someone may get suspicious." "Okay, all right" Will interrupted. "When will you be finished everything. When will you be completely loaded?" "Well", Art paused to think. "Now that everyone's back from holiday it should not take more than two weeks." "Okay thanks man, keep me posted." "Will don't give up, you know what they say, "It ain't over till" "Yeah, yeah". Will cut in again "Till the fat lady sings. Talk to you later Art"

As Will was pulling the covers back over his head, Matt was getting up. It was his first day on the new job at America's Pulse. Harold Nelson was a legend there and his shoes will be hard to fill. All morning long, a guy in a red pin stripped shirt kept staring at Matt from across the room. "Hey Jim", Matt called him over, "What's the deal with that guy? Is he gay or something what's his deal? He's been staring at me since I got here." "Oh, that's Dave. He's not happy about old man

Nelson retiring. He was like a father to Dave. According to the rumor mill you used your influence upstairs to have Nelson pushed out on account of his age so that you could take his job." "What! That's a lie." Matt was really pissed. "That's a damned lie!" Matt shouted. "Where did you get this crap?" "Calm down Matt. It's just office gossip. Don't let it get to you. Hey, I am on your side. I believe you, but if I were you I would still watch my back around Dave."

It was an election year and in D.C, that meant a lot of political news stories to cover and many photos to go with it. After only two weeks on the job Matt could hear Will's words echoing in his head *"You will be bored to tears within a month if you take this job"*. If Will only knew how true his prediction turned out to be Matt would never hear the end of it.

CHAPTER 3

▼

PAGING SHERLOCK HOLMES

Theresa and Will had a plutonic relationship. It was Saturday night and as head nurse at Walter Reed Hospital, she had to get up early and punch in by 7:00 a.m. Will was home by midnight. He liked the company of the ladies but also enjoyed and valued his privacy. He whispered to himself as he directed the remote toward his stereo system, "I am never alone as long as I have my two friends Marvin Gaye and Johnny Walker to keep me company." After adjusting the volume, he poured a rather large portion of Johnny Walker on the rocks and settled back in his favorite chair. Will's thoughts drifted to the upcoming Spring. He was painfully aware that he would have to pick a new partner or retire from the business of photographing the crop circles. Just minutes later, he would get a call that would make the decision for him.

"Will! Will!" The voice on the other end of the line was unmistakable it was Art. "I've got it! You've done it! I mean *we've* done it." "Art, man slow down. What the hell are you talking about?" "Okay, okay." Art repeated as he tried to relax. Art took a deep breath and he started over. "The computer is going nuts; I mean it is going wild. It's been generating all sorts of charts, maps, numbers, configurations, star charts, and what looks like DNA, and all sorts of crap from the pictures and information that I got from you and Matt. We hit the mother load! As soon as it stops I will be over straightaway mate." *"This is it* "Will thought as he hung up. *"Finally after all these years an answer is coming."* Will's heart began to beat faster. "This is it", he kept repeating to himself.

Art was a bit surprised to see Matt answer Will's door. Will called Matt right after he spoke to Art. Matt lived closer and rushed over as soon as he heard the news. "Wow!" Matt said staring at the two large cardboard boxes that Arthur struggled with. "Where should I put these?" He said while huffing and puffing. "Over there", Will gestured toward the kitchen table. Art dropped the boxes on the table and started back toward the door. "Come on you guys." Art waved frantically, while catching his breath. "There are three more boxes in the trunk and three in the back seat as well, let's go!"

Matt and Will looked stunned. For a few moments they just gazed in amazement at the eight boxes that they hauled in from Art's car. A puzzled Matt turned to Art and said "Are you sure that a few crop circle pictures generated all of this material from your computer?" "Yep, Art replied with a shy grin. "Well mates better put the kettle on; it's going to be a long night."

Will brewed a pot of coffee with the beans that he stored in a tin from their last trip to Mexico. He never mentioned it to Art but Will always believed that tea was a woman's drink. It didn't take long for the men to realize that their treasure chest of information was written in several languages, Chinese, Russian, Spanish and English. It all makes sense, said Matt. "You see, Russia covers the most land. Spanish is the most commonly used language, China has the most people, and we have the technology. Either of you speak Chinese or Russian?" Nor Will or Art bothered to respond. Will and Art began sorting the documents on the coffee table and sofa while Matt decided to use the dinning room table. The remaining boxes were shoved into the corner of the kitchen floor. Matt still seemed baffled and slightly irritated. "What does it all mean? We have diagrams, schematics and solar systems that don't even remotely look like ours." He continued to thumb through the reams of pages. "Look! Formulas, symbols, and only God knows what else are in these boxes. Guys we are in way over our heads. What are we going to do?" Will sat silently on the living room floor staring at the stack of papers that surrounded him. He pondered Matt's question and without looking up he simply said, "Find a common denominator." "What?" Matt turned to Will. "What are you talking about?" Will repeated his answer. "Find a common denominator." Art sprang to his feet. "I get it! We look for a link, a connection, a thread that connects one piece to another; all of this data has to be connected in some way."

After thinking it over a minute Matt said. "The numbers 2400 and the letters A H keep repeating again and again." "I noticed that as well," said Art. "Also, the number 034 and 2012, repeat." Will said, "Except mines has a small circle before the 2400." They all agreed to focus on the documents with the number 2012. 2400. 034. Will left the room and returned with a pen and a small pad. He repeated the numbers as he jotted them down. "2,400. 034. 2,012."And they looked for the letters AH. They came up empty handed and decided to change tactics and look for more clues. Two hours later Matt came up with the outline of the world map. "There was no writing on the map only three digit numbers and lines everywhere. You could clearly see the Pacific and Atlantic oceans." "Hang on fellows." Art was onto something. "If 001 is located in California we could use it as a point of reference. You see it must be because it's closest to the Pacific Ocean. 034 is also three digits…" "I am way ahead of you Art." Will rushed over to his computer and printed out a map about the size and shape of the one that they were looking at. "Bring it over here close to the light." Will placed one map on the top of the other and held them up to the light. "Well, if your theory is correct 034 is somewhere in England. Maybe this is some sort of meeting place," said Matt. They went back to the numbers again. "Look at the o before the 2400." What? said Arthur. "I don't see anything." Matt began to smile. "It's too perfect. It's not an O; it's a symbol for the sun or the moon. Since it's so obvious that the Aliens don't want to be seen I am betting that the O symbolizes the moon." "Of course!", Will cut in, "2400 is 12 midnight military time." "Since it is a complete circle not a half or a quarter the Aliens have probably been showing up when the moon is full." Art was not convinced. "Hold on, hold on. How do we know that we are dealing with Aliens?" "Who else could it be said Matt. Who or what else has the ability to produce all of those elaborate Crop Circles and all of this stuff?" Art held the maps up to the light to see for himself. "Okay, if you are right 001maybe the San Andreas Fault line in California. There are no major fault lines in that part of Jolly O' England near 034." "None to speak of but there are some major land or lay lines you know magnetic energy lines but…" Before Art could finish his sentence Will was already back at the computer conducting a Google search for lay lines in England. "Got it!", Will shouted, "Stonehenge. That's got to be where aliens will land on the next full moon." Matt rushed to the calendar on the kitchen wall. "The next full moon is in three days. That does not give us much time." "Wait a minute guys. We are forgetting something. What about 2012 and the letters AH huh? We still don't know what they mean." "Well, maybe the ET's can tell us when we meet them at Stonehenge," said Will. Matt and Will were so pleased with their discovery that they didn't notice that Art was no longer part of the conversation. He sat quietly at the kitchen table in deep thought as his eyes lay fixed on the chart that was on the table in front of him. Art began tapping on the paper. Finally in a voice barely above a whisper he spoke. "The aliens won't be at Stonehenge." Matt and Will were in the living room and did not hear him. Art spoke again this time in a loud voice. "The aliens won't be waiting at Stonehenge. AH, AH, they will be landing at Aubrey Hedge."

Seven hours and three very strong pots of coffee later the trio had solved the first small fraction of a very long and confusing puzzle. They were completely oblivious to the fact that it was now Sunday morning and many people were already on their way to church or work. After working through the night Art, Will, and Matt's spirits were flying high. Maybe it was from all that Mexican coffee or maybe it was the fact that on Wednesday, February 7th they would come face to face with visitors from another planet. Through all of the excitement there was still one burning question that stood out from the rest. What was the significance of the numbers Two Zero One Two?

CHAPTER 4

▼

CLOSE ENCOUNTERS OF THE THIRD KIND

"Yo Matt, this is Will, I am on the cell outside of your window." Matt's desk at the magazine was close to the window on the seventh floor. He could see Will waving something that looked like papers but could not make out what it was. "Be right down Will." Matt grabbed his jacked off the back of the chair and headed for the bank of elevators unaware that Dave had been watching his every move from across the busy room. The moment Matt left Dave quickly rushed over to the window to where Matt had stood moments ago. He waited and watched until he saw Matt approach a black man leaning on a dark blue late model car that was double-parked. He was too far away to hear the conversation or to see what was written on the envelope that was handed to Matt by the stranger standing at the car.

Dave's mind went into overdrive. "What could it be?" He thought. "A payoff of some kind? Drugs? Blackmail? Or maybe a lead on a hot story, a scoop." It was no secret that Dave did not like Matt and wanted to have him fired. Dave was convinced that Matt was shady and that the proof was in that envelope. When Matt returned to his desk, he placed his jacket on the back of the chair. Dave could see the corner of the envelope peeking out from the inside pocket. Dave wanted to run over and just rip it open to find out what was inside but instead he decided to call in a favor from an old friend upstairs in personnel. A few minutes later Matt received a called from upstairs to fill out a few "BS" forms that Dave's friend used to lure Matt away from his desk. Before Matt was on the elevator Dave had retrieved the envelope and had his curiosity satisfied. "Roundtrip airline tickets to London", he murmured. "This could be that break that I have been waiting for." He carefully copied all for the information from the ticket and quickly put everything back exactly as he had found it.

"Here we are." Matt pointed to the United Airlines Flight #2830 on the departure screen as they walked down the concourse. "I sure miss the Concord", gripped Art as he struggled with his luggage while trying to keep up with Will and Matt who were used to packing light. "Going home was far simpler than it is now. A quick trip on the shuttle to New York, hop on the Concord and before you know it you're there." The three decided not to risk talking about the nature of the trip until they reach the hotel where they could speak freely. After two connections and a equipment delay Matt could see the Thames River from his window seat as the plane came in for a landing. Among the crowds of people milling about in the airport lounge was a man peering from behind a copy of the London Times. He followed the men to the hotel. The stalker instructed the cab driver to keep his distance in order to keep from being noticed. The man entered the hotel but ducked into the gift shop just off the main lobby to purchased an instant camera. As soon as he was sure that he had not been spotted, he returned to the cab waiting up the street.

Later that night, with Arthur behind the wheel, the three traveled in the car they had rented earlier up to Avebury henge unaware that they were still being followed. "Here we are", said Art as he pulled the car over to the shoulder of the dark and lonely road. "We should walk from here. The main part of the hedge is just over that ridge." When they reached the center they scouted the area to be certain that they were not being followed. Matt glanced at his watch. "12:14 our friends are a no-show, or maybe we made a mistake in our calculations." "No, no", said Art. "I am certain that we are at the proper place at the right time. I have checked over those documents a hundred times. This is the place all right." "Maybe we were just wrong. Maybe they aren't any aliens." Matt speculated. "Wait!" Art held his index finger in the air. "Do you smell that guys?" Will turned up his nose. "Smells like rotten eggs to me", he said. Art turned to Will and Matt. "Not eggs, sulfur. And it's coming from that direction." Art began running like a bloodhound that just picked up a scent. In mid-stride, he ran into something that knocked him out cold.

"What the hell!" Matt shouted. He looked at Will and they both looked at Art lying on the frozen ground. There was nothing in sight. They rushed over to help their friend, who lay motionless in the field. As they knelt down Will placed his hand on the ground for balance. "Yo Matt, something really strange is going on here. The ground is vibrating." At that moment a light haze of lime green mist began to form around them. Before they could decide what to do a shinny jet-black craft appeared before them right next to Art. The mist grew thicker but they could still notice the dim light from the door slowly opening on the right side of the spacecraft. Two tall male forms walked from the ship toward them. This was it. It was obvious from their attire that they were not from this world. One of the men began to speak. "I bid you peace. You have no idea how long we have waited for this moment to arrive." Will and Matt stood motionless and speechless. "Your friend is injured, allow us to help." One of the aliens had dark blue hair, when he moved away from the light it actually looked black. He motioned toward Art. When they did not respond he carried Art inside the ship. The other alien was a little shorter with shoulder length redish brown hair. The shorter man did not speak but motioned for Matt and Will follow. Once on the ship the door closed behind them and once again the ship seemed to vanish. Matt and Will were not the only ones amazed at the dramatic arrival of the aliens, the man who had shadowed them since their arrival at the airport was back. This time he watched, with high-powered binoculars from a clump of trees on the other side of the clearing. The stalker had shed his disguise. He would be much easier for Matt to recognize. It was Matt's nemesis, Dave.

The interior of the ship was bathed in the same green light that was seen outside the ship. "Lay him on the table", said one of the aliens. The taller of the two aliens operated a machine over head. It made a humming noise and in a few minutes, Arthur was up and about. "What happened?" he asked. "Tell ya later." Will said. "Please have a seat." The alien motioned to the metallic chairs nearby. "We are most pleased that you were finally able to decipher the crude messages that we have been sending over the years. We have much to discuss and there is very little time. Please do not be deceived by our humanoid appearance. The fact that you are here indicates your realization that we are not of this world. I am Mr. Gray said the taller man, and this is Mr. Blue of course these are not our true birth names, but we have learned from monitoring your world that misplaced trust often leads to betrayal. You see we are not authorized to be here. In point of fact is it's forbidden. We have monitored your conversation for the past twenty-three minutes. You are Matthew, Will, and Arthur." The shorter alien Mr. Blue cut in. "We belong to an outlawed organization called Earth's Guardians 2." Will raised his hand as if he was sitting in class. "Excuse me, what happened to the first guardians of Earth?" Mr. Blue turned to Will and said, "They were discovered and sent into exile." "Banished?" "Why? And by whom?" Will asked.

"Years ago, the Planetary Alliance voted nine to eight against saving Earth's people from destruction. They believed that your spices was far too violent to co-exist in the cosmos." "Stop! Wait a minute." Arthur leaped from his seat followed by Matt and Will. "Earth's destruction! You are speaking figuratively right?" "No." said Mr. Grey. "We assumed that this was the reason you were here. When you read the circles, the timeline was given just as it was told to the Druids, and later to the Aztec's before you. The message was clear. In the 12th month of the year 2012 planet Earth will most certainly be destroyed by a collision with another planet. Recent events indicate that the timeline predicted is accurate." "Eight years." Art slumped to his seat. Matt sat silently. Will was a bit more optimistic. "Wait." He said. "If there is no hope of saving Earth then why are you here?" Mr. Blue spoke. "We never said that there was no hope. The leaders of our planets have consulted the council of Oracles as well as what you call Historians or Grio's. Many, many years ago, the Chief Oracle foretold the breakaway of the planet Otar from the Alliance. This event, which has recently taken place, has shifted the vote to save earth from 9-8 to 8-8. The deadlock could not be broken so it was decided that your fate would be determined by your intelligence." Matt was pissed. "Are you trying to tell me that billions of people may be wiped out if we don't pass your IQ test?"

"We are of one mind" Mr. Grey said as he moved his hand around the room in a circular motion. "Earth cannot be saved but the people of Earth can. We began sending our messages secretly embedded with the more complex messages of our leaders. A planet has been prepared for you and your people. You see the planet that broke away from the alliance has triggered a chain of events that will lead to the destruction of Earth. Please be patient your questions will be answered." Again, Mr. Blue picks up the story.

"The planetary alliance controls many uninhabited plants; each planet in the Alliance has an equal number of planets suitable for terra forming. In simple terms, we posses the technology to convert or transform a lifeless planet into whatever type planet is require. When Otar broke from the alliance of Planets they not only forfeited their allotment of planets, they also were denied the technology to terra form. They have since found a new far more radical terra-forming program. All of there previous attempts have gone awry and have produced devastating results. The council of Oracles from the sixteen planetary alliances have been in agreement for thousands of years that out of desperation Otar's future attempt to terra form will result in a catastrophe so huge that the planet involved will rip though the space portal with such force that it will hurl itself completely out of control until it hits a planet called Earth in the year 2012. This is the only time in the history of our civilization that every single Oracle including the Chief has been in complete agreement. Earth must be evacuated in order for the human race to survive. The hours have grown short. This process should have begun at least six Earth years ago. The Alliance of Planets has prepared an Earth like Planet in another solar system as a new home for you and your people. In accordance with our Galactic laws if the humans do not take possession within the ten years Time Of Habitation rule the Otarians will surely stake its claim of the new planet by means of having the planet declared abandoned. Each day they become more and more desperate. Because of the radical laws that were put into place by the Otarians their planets have become dangerously over crowded. They believed that the rules of the alliance were too rigid. Once their planet gained independence and became a sovereign planet their population quickly began to spiral out of control."

"This is too much to absorb", said Will shaking his head while pacing up and down the small isle of the craft. "It's like a dream, a really bad dream." "More like a nightmare", muttered Matt under his breath. "Just how are we supposed to get to this so-called New Earth?" Mr. Blue slowly waved his hand across the screen to his right. A solar system with eleven planets appeared on the monitor. "Here is your new home", he announced with a hint of pride in his voice. He pointed to the blue planet on the solar chart Earth 2. "You have been supplied with all that is required to save yourselves. Deep space charts, ships, diagrams, factory diagrams, nutritional plans, fuel preparations etc. As you Earthlings are fond of saying we have given you the works. Your navigators will have to learn the basics in order to guide the ships out of Earth's atmosphere. With the exception of take off and landing the ships have been designed and programmed to take you to your destination by computer automation. This will also prevent anyone from using the crafts for unauthorized trips around the galaxy in the future. In time, your experts will figure out how to build and operate those complex spacecrafts along with the machines and buildings that construct them. But since time is the one thing that you do not have Earth's Guardians have sent you the key." Mr. Blue asks Mr. Grey to continue. "Each member of Earth's Guardians has spent many years learning the thousands of compounds involved in constructing and operating the massive factories and the space ships they build. As individuals their knowledge is useless. If anyone of our members were discovered the authorities would consider their knowledge unimportant and would dismiss it as mere curiosity. Our space technology is far more advanced then any system every created and for that reason it has been protected vigorously", said Mr. Blue. "The collective knowledge of our Guardians working on this project contains everything you need to know including building factories, and ships; also how to read Star charts and everything you require to guide your people to safety was transferred into the mind of Mr. Grey. He is the possessor of the key. In order to expedite the ship building process and increase your odds of evacuating on time he will now transfer this knowledge to one of you." Matt was skeptical to say the least. "How is this possible? And why would you and your people or whatever you call yourselves risk exile for a planet full of strangers." "Mr. Grey, please answer the man's question." "You see thousands of years ago one of our ships crashed landed one night not far from this location. The crew was badly injured, barely alive, and the ship was in need of major repairs. The Druids, a name they created for themselves, concealed the craft and provided refuge to our people. For many months they tended to the injuries of the crew until they were able to walk and repair their ship. As a gesture of thanks and good will, they used the technology abroad the ship to construct a celestial place of worship for the Druids. This story has been passed down through the ages. I believe they called it the Hedge of Stone." "Mr. Blue the energy level on the cloak is declining we must soon return to the ship." "You mean this is not your ship?" said Matt. "No, we are Star Charters you would call us mapmakers by profession. This is just our shuttle. We must leave this place soon before we are detected. Who wishes to undergo the Transfer of Knowledge?"

After a brief discussion, Matt reluctantly agreed to participate in what the aliens called the Accelerated Mind Transfer or AMT for short. Mr. Grey dimmed the lights in the cabin of the shuttle with just a wave of his hand while Mr. Blue passed Matt a small metal cup that contained what looks like hot green herb tea. He took a sniff. "The aroma was very strong, pungent and intoxicating. Drink slowly please." Matt sipped the tea slowly as Mr. Blue had instructed while Will and Art looked on. It did not take long for the strange brew to kick in. The elixir made Matt feel woozy and warm all over. Grey sat across the table from Matt. He instructed Matt in a soft calming voice. "Do exactly as I do." He grabbed Matt's left hand from across the table and held it tight. Matt squeezed back. Then he placed the palm of his right hand onto Matt's forehead and closed his eyes. Matt repeated the movements made by Mr. Grey exactly. Will and Art stood on the sidelines waiting to see what was going to happen next. Art could not help but notice that there was no lifeline in the palm of Mr. Grey's hand. He could only catch a quick glimpse of what appeared to be in an infinity symbol. "Curious."

He found himself saying aloud. "What's curious?" Will asked. "Shh. I will tell you later."

"Nothing's happening", said Matt. "Quiet." said Mr. Blue "an AMT has never been preformed on a human before. We must be patient." A few seconds later thousands of images began to bombard Matt's mind from all direction in all shapes colors and sizes. Afterwards strange letters, numbers, documents, and voices that sounded like gibberish came to his mind. Matt was no longer in control. He felt helpless and vulnerable. Had it not been for the calming affects of the tea he probably would have freaked out. What seemed like hours to Matt was actually about two minutes. Matt held on until the very end then collapsed to the floor. "Help him up", said Mr. Blue. "He's going to be fine. Just give him a few minutes to recover. The transfer has apparently been a success."

Beep! Beep! Beep! "We have an intruder on the grounds and the shield is beginning to fail." Mr. Grey turned to Will and Art. "Have you brought anyone else with you?" "No! It's just the three of us. "Will responded. "The cloak is down. We are visible!" shouted Mr. Blue. Mr. Grey turned to a second screen. "There is a human headed away from the ship toward the wooded area. We must leave before he returns with more humans. It is no longer safe to meet here. We will meet again the same time next month at Henge of Stone in the United States." Mr. Grey could tell from Art's expression that he had no idea of where the new meeting place was. Anticipating the question from Art Mr. Grey said "North Salem, New Hampshire." Art nodded thanks. Matt had begun to regain control over his motor functions but still needed a little help from his friends. Their new alien friends waved goodbye and wished them luck as they helped Matt down the ramp and back to the car. By the time they reached the car Matt had fully recovered.

"Hey!" Matt patted his pockets. "My candy, my candy bar is gone. I must have dropped it when I passed out on the ship." Matt's candy was not all that was gone. Matt's co-worker Dave was gone too, but not before, he was able to snap a few pictures of the alien space ship.

CHAPTER 5

▼

PITFALLS

Arthur, Will and Matt spent most of the night back at the hotel trying to wrap their minds around what they had just experienced. It was hard, to come to grips with what they learned about the coming demise of Earth and how they might be able to pass the tragic information on to the government authorities without being labeled kooks or whack jobs. "Can't mention aliens", said Matt. "The second you do they are going to start thinking little green men and put us in a padded room. Let's just give them the data that we got from Art's computer. If they buy it then we can tell them the rest. Everything except about tonight's meeting." Will took a sip of cola and put the glass on the table. "Okay Einstein, how are we going to get to someone at the top? You know, someone with clout. Don't forget what the man said, we are running out of time. We don't have the luxury of waiting around for some low level suits to go through the proper channels." "I don't know", Art said quietly. "This is all happening so fast." He looked at Will and Matt. "I will tell you this much. If we don't do something really quick we are all screwed. Not just England and America but the whole ball of wax. Game over. Not to mention whoever was lurking about outside the ship. I can't believe that this is real. I am expecting to wake up right now." That morning after staying up all night, the three made their way through the airport terminal. Art was pre-occupied with what happened during last night's encounter and was not paying much attention to where he was walking. He bumped the shoulder of a stunning dark haired woman. "Sorry" he said without even looking to see whom he had just run into. "Artie? Artie, is that you?" The voice was unforgettable. It was Art's college sweetheart, Julie Skinner. Art's mood suddenly brightened up. "Hello Julie", what a surprise. "How are you? How's the fashion biz?" "I'm great, and business could not be better. How about you Artie? How are things in America?" "Very busy these days." As Julie adjusted her purse Art noticed that she was not wearing a wedding ring. Last he heard she was engaged to some French guy. He decided to take a chance. "How's your husband?" Julie looked Art straight in the eyes and smiled. "Oh, Jacques. Things between us just didn't work out. The wedding was called off." Jackpot! Exactly what I was hoping for, thought Art. He could tell from the look in her eyes that the magic was still there. Matt looked at his watch. "Come on Artie, we are going to miss our flight." Art knew that the guys would never let the Artie thing go. Julie was the only one who had ever called him by that name. "I have a buyers meeting in New York next month. Maybe I could swing by D.C after the meeting and we could catch up. Here's my number. Give me a call if you are not busy." Wow! This just keeps getting better and better", Art said to himself as he walked toward Matt and Will.

Julie and Art went to their separate ways after college. She went to France to pursue a career in designing women's clothing and Art headed to the states for Technology. It was a friendly split but it is clear that they were by no means over each other. Art sat on the plane a happy man. For the moment thoughts of the end of the world were not as important.

When Matt pulled into his driveway, he noticed a police car parked in front of his door. He slammed the gearshift into park and ran over to the patrol car without bothering to shut his car door. "Good morning officer, is there a problem?" The policeman glanced down at his note pad. "Are you Matthew Matteo?" "Yes, I am. What's going on?" "Mr. Matteo there was a break in at you residence late last night. Your wife was attacked and injured by an intruder. She has been taken to Memorial Hospital; I have been given instructions…" Before he could finish his next sentence Matt was back in his car. He raced down the street like a bat out of hell.

Sara was unconscious when the paramedics brought her in. The neighbors had heard her screams last night and called the police. She regained consciousness an hour or so after Matt arrived. Slowly, she opened her eyes. "Matt, where am I?" "You're in the hospital. A burglar attacked you last night. I am sorry babe. How do you feel? Should I call the nurse?" She smiled and said it's not your fault. Just then the nurse entered the room and called the doctors. The doctor ask Matt to wait outside but called him into the room after the examination and test results had come back. His face was grim. "Mr. and Mrs. Matteo I am afraid I have some bad news: You have lost the baby. I am so sorry." Sara began to weep; but Matt was devastated. "No! It can't be right. How? You've got to run more test." "Our tests are conclusive. Your wife was pushed down a flight of steps as indicated by the location of her bruises and the sprain on her left hand that she used to break her fall. That was enough to, he paused, to....the child was not able to withstand the fall", he finished.

Matt fought back the tears. He could not look Sara in the eyes. His range of emotions was difficult to control guilt, anger, helplessness, rage, but most of all compassion for Sara. "I am so sorry" the doctor spoke again. "I think you two need some time alone to sort things out. I will stop back in a half hour." Matt rushed over to console Sara. He blamed himself for the death of their child. He kept saying over and over, "I should have been there; I should have been there."

Will was not aware of what was going on with Matt and Sara. After a few hours sleep he hooked up with Art for lunch. "This is very risky", said Art. Will stared nervously at him. "It's the only chance we have. Look, we write the letter giving as much information as we can without revealing our identities and Matt will slip it into the pocket of one of the President's aids at the campaign stop next week." "But what if he gets caught?" Art insisted. "Or suppose President Walker doesn't get the message until after the press conference? What then?" Seeing Will's frustration Arthur decided to back off. "If the plan worked the President would include the phrase "we need to solve this problem now" in his remarks. This would indicate that he received the letter and was willing to send a representative to the café to set up the meeting." Will folded the letter after Art made a few changes to the wording.

Later that evening after not being able to reach Matt at home Will called to Matt's cell phone. "Hey man, what's up? I have been trying to get you all day. The letter is ready to go. You want me to drop it off?" "No", said Matt. "I'm out." "Out?" Will repeated. "What do you mean out? Are you high?" Matt broke the bad news. "Sara's in the hospital we lost the baby." "Damn! What happened?" Matt was starting to lose it again and Will could hear it in his voice. "Where are you Matt?"

Twenty minutes later, Will arrived at the hospital. Matt was a mess. "Come on Matt let's take a walk." Matt reluctantly left with Will to sit in the cafeteria. It was late and the place was almost empty. "Let's sit over here in the corner." Will handed Matt his coffee. "Looks like we are going to push things back a few weeks huh", Matt? "The aliens who voted not to save the Earth had it right", said Matt. "Maybe this is God's way of telling us that our society is too barbaric and we don't deserve to live. Just like Sodom and Gomorra but on a larger scale." "Come on Matt." Will said softly, "that's your grief talking. You just need a…" "No!" Matt pounded the table with his fist. "I don't give a damn what happens! I am out! It's over!" Matt got up and walked away.

Early next morning Will told Arthur about the loss of the baby and Matt's decision to quit the team. Will had decided to deliver the letter himself. He remembered how a woman looking for a job slipped her resume in President Clinton's pocket when he campaigned for President. "Well", Will said to his self "if it worked for her I guess it could work for me."

It felt like the coldest day of the year and the wind did not help any. Will stood at the rope line early so that he could be up front. "I am standing here in the frigging cold to save this rock." Will continued to muttering, "Why didn't this happen in July? I am freezing my nuts off."

After what seemed like an eternity, President Richard Walker came into view. Will was shaking and this time it wasn't from the cold. As the President stopped in front of him, he shook his hand and began to slip the letter out of his pocket when he felt a large handgrip on his shoulder while another hand snatched the letter from him. Someone yelled "Anthrax!" and all hell broke loose. Will was forced to the ground face down first. He could hear people screaming and running as the secret service hustled President Walker back into the limo.

Later that day, bruised and battered Will sat under heavy guard in a small cell pissed, not with the secret service but with himself. There was one major flaw in his plan: No one had ever heard of Anthrax during the Clinton Presidency in the mid 90s.

Arthur and Matt saw what happened to Will on the news but Art still was not able to convince Matt to help get Will out. "Will's a survivor", Matt confidently said. "He grew up on the streets of Philly, the part you didn't venture into after dark unless you knew how to defend yourself. He'll be alright." "What about you, Matt? How are you and Sara holding up?" "It's still rough." He shrugged his shoulders. "I won't leave her alone. My mom or sister comes over before I go to work."

Arthur was on his own. No one had heard from Will since his arrest. No phone calls, no hearing, and nothing in the media. Will was kept isolated, not in a cell but in a room. He was not interrogated but interviewed by several different men each with a copy of his letter. Something was definitely up. For weeks the questioning continued. Then one day things began to fall into place. One of the men began talking about Groom Lake. Will's inquisitors did not believe his stories about the crop circles, but they did believe that he could lead them to the aliens so they could gain knowledge of their technology.

Arthur was the only one to greet his Alien friends on the next full moon. "I am T'zar and this is Onan. The fact that you are here alone without the government authorities has shown us that you are a trustworthy human. What progress have you to report and where are your companions?" Art explained the sad state of affairs to his alien friends. Onan and T'zar huddled in the corner and began to whisper. When they finished they turned to Arthur and T'zar said, "You require proof. Once you do you will surly be taken seriously. Will will be released and your people can proceed. One week from tomorrow an experiment will be conducted by the Otarians on the planet you call Mars." T'zar then pointed to an instrument that looked like a clock with four hands of various lengths and sizes. Art could not make out any of the symbols. "According to the Chief Oracle at exactly 2:17 p.m. Mars will experience a huge explosion. Relay this information to your people and your voice will be heard." Onan handed Arthur a small metal box. "T'zar and I have decided that it is no longer safe to travel to your planet. Inside this box are three communication devices. On the week of the full moon, we will be in range but will not land unless you require our assistance. Please guard them carefully." Art reached for the box. "Thank you, for everything."

"During our last visit you left behind chocolate." "Oh yes," Art recalled Matt's candy bar. "We were wondering if perhaps you or your companions Will or Matt could bring more the next time we meet. We are willing to compensate you." Arthur laughed, "You risk your lives to save our planet and all you want in return is chocolate candy?" He was meeting Julie in three days. Julie loved Hershey Kisses so her picked up a bag on the way to meeting his alien friends. "Hang on," Art told his friends. "I'll be right back." A few minutes later, he returned with the bag of Kisses. Here you are, enjoy. T'zar and Onan thanked Art for the candy and wished him luck.

Meanwhile back in D.C., Matt had begun having dreams. Dreams he could not share with Sara because they were vivid pictures of people and places from the home world of the aliens. After the accident, Matt decided that he would not tell Sara the truth about his trip to England. She did not know about the meeting with the aliens. After weeks of dreams, Matt concluded that he had been given some of Mr. Gray's personal memories along with the information of saving Earth. With every dream he had Matt's knowledge of this stranger grew and became more vivid. He felt as though he visited the planet but in reality, he didn't even know what it was called.

CHAPTER 6

▼

AN ARMY OF ONE

Three days had passed since Art's meeting with his alien friends. As he stood on the platform waiting for Julie's train to arrive, he began feeling a bit selfish. *The fate of the entire human race is in my hands*, he thought. *I have only a mere 6 days to conceive and implement a plan to alert the President about the Mars explosion and get Will released. Poor bastard is probably rotting away in some hell hole while I am standing here trying to figure out how to get Julie up to my flat so that I can get into her knickers. I really must work on my priorities.*

As the Amtrak train pulled into the crowded station Art's heart began beating harder. The passengers slowly began to pour out of the train but there was no sign of Julie. Art noticed a rather large man with a beard wearing a suit at least two sizes too small for him heading his way. When the man stopped to look at the signs overhead a tall slender women sidestepped her way around him. It was a welcoming sight. It was Julie. Art rushed over to help her with her bags. "Thought you backed out on me." said Art with a huge grin. "Not a chance" she replied smiling in return. "I am not going to loose you again." she continued. "Oh, I brought you something." Art handed her the chocolate candy that replaced the candy, from his meeting with Onan and T'zar. "Oh Artie, you remembered. This is so sweet of you." She held up the bag of kisses and said "One Kiss deservers another." She gave Art a kiss on the cheek. Art pointed to the candy and replied, "There must be at least thirty Kisses in that bag by my modest calculation you still owe me twenty nine more." "In due time young man.

Remember patience is a virtue." They both had a good laugh and headed out of the station.

Julie's hotel suite turned out to be a waste of hard-earned cash. With the exception of popping in for a quick change of clothes, she was hardly ever there. She spent most of her time out on the town with Art. Concerts, movies, the theatre, restaurants, shopping, and late night chats. They were inseparable. Art wanted to tell Julie all about his alien encounters but everything was going so well that he decided not to. He did not want to freak her out and spoil the mood. They were officially a couple again. For three wonderful days, Art was able to put the troubles of the world aside. Julie was probably the only person on earth that could have that effect on him. The day had come that Art dreaded. *Where did the time go?* He wondered. He waved as Julie boarded the United Airlines flight for a designer's convention. In a strange way, Julie's visit helped him to focus. Life was okay before their chance encounter but now…now he had something to live for. His reunion with Julie was just the motivation he needed to get him going.

From his vantage point, Matt watched the lunch crowd thin out as most of the suits got back to work. He chose the last booth way in the back, so that he could see Art when he entered. Just as he decided to order, Art walked thru the door. "Good to see ya, Matt." They shook hands and sat down. "Thanks for agreeing to meet with me Matt." Matt was curious to know what Art was carrying in the briefcase that lay in the seat next to him but was determined not to ask.

"How's Sara been?" "Sara's doing better she's out shopping with her mother. Look Arthur I appreciate your concern but you could have asked me that over the phone. Why did you ask me to meet you here?" Arthur took a deep breath and began to speak in a whisper. "I have a plan to get Will out. Before you say anything let me finish. I am not going to ask you to get involved and I won't even tell you what I intend to do, if you don't want to know. I realized it the other day when Julie came to town." Matt started to grin, "you mean the girl from the airport? Son of a gun!" "Yes," Art replied, "she almost found this in my closet. I need you to hold on to this in case I end up with Will. You have a house. It should be easier to hide it there." He handed Matt the case. Matt stared at the briefcase regretting his earlier curiosity over its contents. He looked around then opened it. "Are these what I think they are?" "Yes," said Art sill whispering. "There is no risk on your part since no one knows they exist but me, and I have no reason to rat you out." "Okay, I'll do it!" "What?" Art was dumbfounded. "You what?" Matt closed the case and laid it beside him. "I said that I would do it. Why you want it back?", said Matt. "No, no." Art shook his head, "its just that I thought that I would have to beg and maybe grovel a little first. Why the change of heart?" "Okay Art I have a confession to make. You said that you hadn't told Julie about our friends from out of town well Sara is still in the dark too. You are the only one left to tell." "Tell what?" Said Art. "About the dreams I've been having. Just about every night, only I don't think they are dreams, they are more like memories." Arthur waved his hand back and forth while leaning on the table. "Stop! Are you trying to tell me that T'zar transferred his memory into your mind?" "Not transferred," said Matt "duplicated is more like it, and not everything. Just fragments, you know places and events. One night I dreamed that I was sitting on a hill top over looking a village but the sky slowly turned from a powder pink to a light orange color and to my left were two more planets." "Wow!" Was all Art could say, as he listened in amazement. "Last night I was in what looked like a forest. There was a gentle breeze blowing. When it flowed through the leaves it sounded like the trees were singing. It was beautiful. I can't read their writing but last week I saw what must have been some kind of festival. At first it was pitch dark and all you could hear was music, then there were the flickering globes painted in bright vivid colors lit by the candles placed inside and there were boats, hundreds of boats with the flickers globes on board. There was music, singing, and the smell of unusual food as the boats made their way around an island. That?s incredible shouted Art, realizing that they had drawn the attention of the folks a few seats away he lowered his voice. No wonder you could not tell your wife.

The waitress returned with Matt's lunch. While she was taking Art's order four guys in business suites sat in the booth right next to theirs. The fact of the matter is that they are regulars and they sit there everyday. Not wanting to take any chances. Matt and Art spent the rest of lunch making small talk.

CHAPTER 7

▼

THE BIG BANG

With only one day left Arthur began to put his plan into motion. Using relays and aliases to cover his tracks, Art hacked into the computers for Homeland Security and the CIA. After locating the e-mail addresses of both directors he began talking to himself as he often does when he gets nervous. "Okay, here we go. The e-mail message said our planet is about to be destroyed." "No, no, no." Art started mumbling again. "Millions of people in America are in danger. You have been holding a man named William Johnson. The letter that he tried to give President Walker is real. If you want proof come to this private chat room at noon tomorrow. Save the Homeland USA." Arthur hit send and logged off. He looked around the small internet café to see if he had been noticed. Good no one even looked up. They were pre-occupied with their surfing. Art was shaking. *I'd better get the hell out of here*, he thought.

Art did not sleep much that night. He talked to Julie over the phone around eleven o'clock at night, then spent most of the night going over the plan several times. Talking to Julie somehow gave him the confidence he needed to pull off the final phase of his plan. If they read his e-mails they would be waiting, not just in that chat room but waiting to trap him and bring him in.

The day seemed like any other. It was a bright sunny morning with a brisk cold breeze. People went about their daily routine unaware of the danger that Art was constantly worrying about. At eleven o'clock sharp, Art walked four blocks from his home carrying two small brief cases. He caught a cab downtown. 11:25

a.m. After walking another two blocks, he hailed a second cab and offered the cabbie one hundred dollars for one hour and no questions asked. The driver seemed puzzled but was eager to take the money. Art directed the cab driver to a quite side street where he setup a make shift mobile unit with his laptop that he removed from one of the cases. 11:50 Art gave specific instructions for the cabbie to drive slowly four blocks in each direction ending up across the street from the subway entrance. By 11:55 they were on their way. Art entered the chat room at 12:01 p.m. he did not want to risk being early thus giving them more time to track his signal. He peered through the windows of the back seat before he began to type.

Art: Are you here?
Both of the directors: Yes, who are you?

Arthur expected this tactic. It was meant to keep him online long enough for him to be caught.

Art: My name is not important he replied. We have proof that the Earth will be destroyed Art typed. Have you spoken to Will?
Homeland: We have read his letter.
FBI: When can we meet to discuss it?

Art ignored the question. He knew he was running out of time. The palms of his hands were sweating as he typed.

Have you spoken to Will? He repeated.
Homeland: what is your proof? The cabbie had nearly completed his run. Art's timing was critical. He knew that the feds were on their way to his location or at least nearby.
Art: At exactly 2:17 this afternoon, a large explosion will occur on the Planet Mars. The source that provided me with that information is the same source that gave Will and I the details of the pending disaster to take place on Earth.

His time was up. After gathering his equipment and shoving it into the case, he made a beeline to the subway only a few feet away. It was time for the final stage of his carefully thought out plan. The train was right on time, Art made a beeline to the last car. It usually had fewer passengers. He reached in the briefcase and pulled out a hat and a pair of glasses. He put them on, removed the scarf, and packed it away. Art rode to the next stop got off and ran up the stairs.

Meanwhile law enforcement agents surrounded the confused cab driver. "I don't know what you're talking about. "I did nothing wrong. Some guy gave me a hundred bucks to drive him. I don't ask no questions. I just drive. He jumped out a few minutes ago and went down the stairs over there." The agents got Art's description asked a few more questions before letting the cabbie go.

Art headed towards the trash can in the park where earlier this morning he stashed a long over coat wrapped in a plastic bag and hid it in the bottom of the can. He changed coats, removed the hat and glasses then looked around to see if anyone noticed. It was freezing cold; the only living creatures in the park besides Art were a few hungry pigeons. The pounding in Art's chest had begun to subside. *I think I may have pulled it off.* Arthur said to himself. He was nervously confident. Art stashed the two cases in the locker at a nearby bus terminal. Too afraid to go home he went to the local pub where the bar tender always watched the cable news.

It was 12:50 p.m. Art ordered a pint and sipped slowly his eyes alternating between the T.V. and the front door in case they did come looking for him there. Minutes seemed like hours. 2:17 came and went but still no word. Art began to doubt the accuracy of the information given to him by his alien friends. He thought: *One more hour and I'm going to check into the Holiday Inn. Not safe to go home not knowing what's going on.* When Art came from the bathroom, several people were already gathered around the T.V. "I repeat said the T.V. anchorman shortly after two o'clock p.m. East coast time there was a massive explosion on the planet Mars. Scientist and astronomers are at a loss as to what caused this event." Art's eyes were glued to the TV set. For the first time since this odyssey had begun the realization of what was to follow had finally sunk in. He knew if they were right about Mars that they would also be right about Earth.

The folks at the pub were not the only ones watching the event unfold on Mars, across town at America's Pulse everyone's attention was focused on the three screens mounted on the walls of the magazines main room. By now CNN, MSNBC, and FOX were all reporting the story. While the workers stopped to watch the screen, Dave watched Matt. Dave was a writer not a photographer. For weeks, he tried to sell his space ship pictures by shopping them around under his alias but had no takers. Not even the tabloids were interested. The response was always the same too burly, too dark, or too far away. Dave felt that somehow, some way Matt was involved with the explosion on Mars. After watching the news Art felt more confident about going home. He walked to his car and drove to his street. He parked a few doors away and waited to see if there was anyone lurking about. As Art began to doze off the ringing of his cell phone startled him.

It was Will. "Art, this is Will, what's been going on? What did you do?" He sounded happy. "Will! Where are you? Are you out?" In spite of the fridge cold Art got out of the car and paced up and down the sidewalk as he talked. This was the call he had waited for so long. "Yea man", Will answered. "They have been acting very strange. Flew me back on a private jet." "Is that right?" said Art. "What do you mean by strange?" "Man the feds have been kissing my butt all afternoon; asking lots of questions about the aliens, spaceships, and something about blowing up Mars. I think they finally believe us Art. I don't know why or how, but they do. Can you meet me at my place? I need to make a few calls to let people know that I'm okay." "Sure Will, I will be there in twenty minutes." Will's place was in disarray. Everything had been tossed about but nothing had been broken. Instead of the usual handshake Art and Will hugged one another and slapped each other on the back. "Great to see you mate. What the hell happened here?" "Damn Feds", Will waved his hand in disgust. "As far as I can tell nothing is missing so it must have been the FBI snooping. How are Matt and Sara?" "They are as well as can be expected." Art turned to look Will in the eye, "but how are you Will? Where did they take you?" Will paused and motioned for Art to have a seat. "Where do I begin? Well, first they took me to a holding cell, then to the nut house for a few days. Most of the time they kept me in a room in hanger 18 at Area 51." "Area 51!" Art repeated. Blimy. "Why? I don't know." said Will "but they want to meet with us right away. They said that they received creditable information from a friend of mine. That had to be you." *Knock, knock, knock.* Art looked toward the door. "You expecting company Will?" "No."

Will answered the door. "Good evening I am Agent Wyatt and this is Agent Moore." The two men flashed their badges and ID's. "We have been asked to escort you gentlemen to the White House. Please follow me. Our car is parked out front." Art and Will followed the two agents without question. At last, a meeting with the top Brass. Art could not help wondering if this was a request or a demand. The stoned faced, FBI men could have easily been mistaken for linebackers for the Washington Redskins if it had not been for their tailor made suites. In the back seat, Art caught Will up on events that transpired since his arrest. "Remember Art, show them everything that we have but don't tell them about our friends."

Soon they were sitting face to face with the directors of Homeland Security. The CIA, FBI, Secretary of State, and Secretary of Defense. The CIA director kept staring at Art. "You sure gave our boys a run for their money this afternoon young man. How'd you pull that off? Who helped you?" Art was no longer intimidated. He had found the courage he was lacking earlier in the day. "I am not your problem", Art replied. "You people have a hell of a lot more to worry about than how I gave you the slip." A few minutes later the Vice President entered the room, shook Will and Art's hands and thanked them for coming. The Vice President took control of the meeting. "On behalf of our government I would like to apologize for any inconvenience or mistreatment that we have caused either of you." The Vice President continued. "You can understand how difficult it was to believe your story. I assume that you Mr. Collins, are responsible for alerting us about the explosion on Mars earlier today." "Yes, sir." Art replied. "The Secretary of Defense leaned forward "You mean you claim that you can prove that the destruction of Earth is imminent? Where is your proof?" "In storage", said Art. He placed the silver key on the table and slid it across to the Vice President who handed it to his aide while whispering something into his ear. While everyone waited for the agents to return with the boxes from storage dinner was ordered.

Art and Will proceeded with their story but omitted the parts about Matt and meeting with the aliens. They were bombarded with questions from everyone in the room. It was well into the night before they had convinced everybody in the room that the information was real. The mood turned from somber to one of urgency. "Okay everybody listen up." Vice President Thompson clapped his hands to get everyone's attention in the room. "The information that Mr. Collins and Mr. Johnson have turned over to us covers a massive amount of areas. To top it off, much of it is written in at least three different languages not counting english. People we are well behind the curve on this one. We need to decipher this ASAP. I need linguists, astronomers, chemists, archeologist, scientists, and the people over at Boeing. I need them here within two hours. Mrs. Robinson get NASA on the line." There were more than thirty people in the room. When Thompson gave the word, everyone scattered with cell phones, PDA's and Blackberries in hand..

The Vice President completed a few calls and came over to Will and Art. "You guys look beat. My assistant will get you settled in your rooms where you can get some sleep. We owe you two a great debt. I will see you in the morning. Thank You." He shook their hands and introduced them to a tall slender woman who smiled at them before taking them away. "Please, follow me."

Matt's boss big Joe called him in early the next morning. When he arrived at work, everyone was just beginning to assemble around Joe on the main floor. He was a short round heavyset man with a big commanding voice. When he spoke, people listened. "Okay everyone gather round." Joe motioned to the staff as if he were guiding a 747 in for a landing. "Something big is going down at the White

House. Cars have been coming and going all night long. The strange thing is that the President is at the G8 summit in Norway and there is nothing on the wire services or the cable networks. We go to print in seven hours. Check with your sources. We can scoop everybody if we move fast enough. So let's get cracking."

As the crowd dispersed, Matt slowly walked to his desk. As he sat down, he thought *I could save Joe the trouble of running around. I know exactly what went on in the White House, Art and Will have found a way to get their message through.* Matt was relieved. He knew that this was the beginning of the end. *Eventually, they will come for me to retrieve the knowledge given to me by the aliens. They are now the lock and I am the only key.*

CHAPTER 8

▼

EVICTION

It was just after seven a.m. When Art and Will were asked to join the Vice President for breakfast. "Good Morning gentlemen", V.P. Eric Thompson motioned for the two to take their seats at the table. "I thought this would be a good time to bring you guys up to speed." Will and Art were dragging their tails from barely three hours sleep but the V.P. looked fresh and ready to go.

"Art we have contacted your employer and they have promised their full cooperation, unofficially of course. They have also granted you an extended leave. As of forty-five minutes ago, you and Mr. Johnson are on the government's payroll. Here are your temporary Id's; personnel will take care of your photos' later. This alien thing boggles the mind. Our people have been working all night. I am expecting a progress report very soon. If either one of you think of anything else just chime in. I was very impressed with Art's computer knowledge and the way you out-smarted our agents over at Homeland Security when you sent us intelligence on the Mars explosion. By the way Art how did you know about that?"

Before Art could answer, Mrs. Robinson entered the room. "The team is ready Sir; everyone is in the Situation Room." The four made their way down the hall then rode the elevator to sub level four. The V.P. turned to Will and Art and smiled. "I bet you will never see this on any tours of White House special on T.V.", he quipped.

When the elevator doors opened, it was like stepping into another place and time. They stood for a moment in this large cavernous room filled with various types of computers. Some people wore lab coats, some were dressed in military uniforms, and some in street clothes. Everyone was scurrying around, except the two-armed guards stationed on either side of the elevator. Vice President Thompson turned toward Will and said "Hard to believe all of this is built into the bowels of the White House, huh?" Art and Will were very surprised at what they saw. They just started walking forward half-mesmerized by what they were seeing. Five plasma screens each twenty feet high and wide, each was suspended from the ceiling in a semi-circle. On the first screen were flashing images of Easter Island, The White Pyramid, The Mayan Calendar, The Sphinx, Stonehenge, and the Great Pyramid at Giza. The second displayed blueprints and schematics that changed every twenty seconds or so. The third screen flashed various star charts and solar systems in vivid colors. The fourth screen looked similar to the second except you could clearly see that this was no building. It was plans for a mega spacecraft. Symbols that appeared to be complex math equations filled the final screen. Art summarized that it must be for producing fuel to power the vessels. It was all quite amazing. Large speakers and security cameras were spread out through the room. Several long tables were arranged in a semi circle facing the large screens. When the Vice President entered the room everyone sat down at the tables.

"Good morning, everybody." Thompson sat in the center chair and looked left and right as he spoke. "As you are well aware we face a grave situation. President Walker has cut his meeting short as is being fully briefed on his way home. Because time is of the essence, I will proceed in his stead. As a reminder, nothing seen or heard here leaves this room." He turned to the director of Homeland Security. "Bill where do we stand?" "Mr. Vice President, ladies and gentlemen we have been able to decipher and translate roughly thrity five percent of all material received so far by patching into the new super computer at IBT. Here is what we know so far: In the year 2012, eight years from now Earth will collide with an unknown Planet from another solar system rendering it uninhabitable and killing billions of people. Fortunately, our alien benefactors have provided us with the technology to escape this disaster and most important they have given us a new home. Take a look at the third screen. At this point, we don't know how to get there, however we do know on what; hence our mode of transportation. Take a look at screen four." Again Bill pointed and clicked the remote. "According to our preliminary figures we will need between 425 to 500 ships just for the United States."

A four star Army general shouted, "That's not possible. How can we build that many ships in so little time?" Before Bill could answer a small man wearing a white lab coat stood up, took off his glases and shouted "What about the other countries!" "Simmer down" said Bill. "Keep in mind that we have only had this information for less than twenty four hours." Will looked at Art, but felt it was best to keep his mouth shut. Bill continued the briefing as a few people started taking notes. "The journey to our new home will take nine months." The mood of the room was the same as when Art Will and Matt first learned the news. You could see the expressions of shock, and disbelief as Bill turned the briefing over to the man from NASA. "Morning folks, my name is Randy." The forty something blond haired Texan spoke with a slight drawl. "Please focus your attention on screen two. What we have here are the plans to build the factories that will be used to construct the ships. It will take two years to build the factories and about ten months to complete each ship. The ships will be built in parts or modules and constructed; on sites around the countries, such as parks and fields. It would be impossible to build enough factories and ships in time. It is the belief of my team and I, that the airlines and ship building factories should be converted immediately to being constructing the major components needed for the space ships. This will give us a jump-start until the new facilities come online. That's all we have for now." Vice President Thompson leaned back in his chair. "I am very curious about the first screen." A young Asian woman slowly raised her hand. She adjusted her glasses and cleared her throat as if she were stalling. "My name is Susan Kim, I am an archeologist. Thus far, the only connection we have been able to make is from the Mayan Calendar. You see sir the Ancient Mayan's believed that the world would end on December 21, 2012 so this is where their calendar stops. Perhaps they were given this knowledge and choose not to pass it on. We will need more time to determine the significance of the landmarks. Sorry." Thompson leaned forwards and looked around the room. "The survival of the human race is in the hands of each of you in this room. We will meet again in twenty four hours." Around the time, that Marine 1 landed on the lawn of the White House the Washington Post special edition was hitting the street. The headline read: <u>Aliens Serve Eviction Notice to Humans</u>. The news spread worldwide in minutes.

President Walker turned to his Chief of Staff. "How bad is it?" He asked. "Well sir, we are receiving calls from the heads of state and world leaders around the globe. We have no idea of who leaked the story and members of the house and senate are demanding a meeting."

The White House was not the only place flooded with calls. Suddenly Dave's spaceship story didn't seem so far fetched. Later that evening, Dave using his alias had sold his pictures and story to U.S. Today. "It's been a pleasure doing business with you Dave." Dave looked at the check made out for 70,000 **dollars**. "Thank you. I feel vindicated. Everyone laughed a few weeks ago when I **told** them my story." The man smiled at Dave and said, "That will all change **when** tomorrow's edition hits the streets. You do understand that other publications **that** you have spoken to may reveal your identity?" "Yes", Dave nodded, "I am **willing** to take that chance. Thanks again." The two shook hands and went in separate directions.

The morning after the story leaked, events around the White House were moving at light speed. Thousands of reporters gathered from around the world. Cabinet and breakfast meetings with senators and congressional representatives were called. Later that afternoon, the President returned phone calls to many of the world leaders who were in a near panic state. Now it was time to address the nation. President Walker thumbed through the pages, looked into the camera, and began his address. "Good evening, by now you have heard the stories about Earth's evacuation. Much of what you have been told has been pure speculation. Tonight, I will give you the facts. There is absolutely no reason to panic."

"Two days ago we obtained highly classified cryptic information that we are decoding as I speak. The amount of material is vast. At this very moment, hundreds of professionals from various fields are using their expertise to give us the total and complete picture. The rumors that I or any members of my staff have been holding secret meetings with alien beings are totally false. The information that I can share with you, so far is this. One, in approximately eight years earth will be destroyed after colliding with an unknown planet. Two, we now have the capability to produce enough mega spacecrafts to carry every American Man, Woman, and Child to safety. We have knowledge of an uninhabited earthlike planet. I have called for an emergency meeting of the United Nations and the G8 for tomorrow morning where I will present the facts as we know them and share our information with the leaders of the world so that they can make preparations to evacuate their people as well. In the coming days, I will hold a press conference to brief you in more detail. Thank you, and goodnight."

Matt and Sara watched the President's address and the news coverage afterwards. The reporter behind the desk was calm and composed as he spoke. "The President's confirmation of the pending destruction of Earth has triggered mixed reaction around the globe. We are receiving reports of massive street gatherings around the world where people are praying. Some groups are protesting and demanding full disclosure of the facts. I think it is safe to say that the world is stunned by the President's remarks. Many of the world leaders are in route to New York and cannot be reached for comment. Many, more questions remain."

Matt got up from the sofa and started toward the kitchen. "You want something Sara?" Sara stared at Matt. "How can I think of food at a time like this?" She asked. "Aren't you the least bit worried?" Matt tried to act concerned. *How can I tell her that this is old news to me?* He thought to himself. Matt responded with all the fake enthusiasm he could muster. "Course I am concerned babe. What's the point in worrying when you can't do anything about it?" Matt continued on to the kitchen but it wasn't hunger pains he was feeling, it was pangs of guilt. The cold hard truth was that there was plenty he could do if he wanted to.

The world watched and waited around their televisions and radios as the leaders gathered that windy morning in April at the United Nations' building. President Walker spoke for two and a half hours after passing out copies of the documents to his counter parts. Everyone seemed satisfied with the exception of France, Russia, and Germany. They were convinced that the Americans were in contact with the aliens and had conspired with them to stake out the best land for the New United States once they arrived. The Chinese believed that the entire evacuation was a hoax designed to distract other countries while the U.S. continued to move ahead in technology and between Russia, France and Germany. It was decided that they would attempt to contact the aliens and cut a deal for themselves. Two foreign agents were given the task of seeking out the aliens and setting up a meeting. Posing as publishers Gusgoff and Malcolm they were able to setup a meeting with Dave.

To the surprise of the President and his staff, rumors of American's refusing to leave Earth were beginning to grow. At his daily staff meeting, he was informed that the rumors were indeed fact. The Chief of Staff did most of the talking Mr. President a group calling themselves HOPE have already formulated a survival plan. Humans Opposed to Planets Evacuation or HOPE for short. They plan to live underground then rebuild when everything is over. The Vice President entered the room just in time to add to the comments of the Chief of Staff. "Mr. President I have just received word that without more proof of the coming disaster seven countries including France, China, and North Korea will refuse to proceed with the evacuation plan." President Walker was mystified. "Good God man, don't these people know that they are doomed if they stay. Haven't they heard a word that I have said? Locate Will and that computer wiz, maybe we have overlooked something that can get these people to pull their heads out of the sand." The President's mood changed to frustration. With a wave of his hand, his staff responded with a chorus of "Yes Mr. President" as they quickly left the room.

CHAPTER 9

▼

THE THREE AMIGOS REUNITED

A month had gone by since the President shocked the world with his address to the nation. News of the impending disaster had been on the front page everyday. Each Sunday, since the President's address the pews and chairs of every building of worship were packed to the rafters, many churches added additional services to accommodate the new members of the flock. Matt looked forward to Sundays with Sara. It was somewhat of a ritual for them to get cozy on the couch with the Sunday paper while they read and chatted about the week's events. Matt needed the time to take his mind off Dave's death. Looking back, he wondered if things between them could have been better if he had made more of an effort. As he reached down to pick up the paper from off the front lawn he noticed a black GTO parked near the corner. The same car was parked in the lot of his job two days ago. When the two men inside the car realized that Matt had spotted them they quickly speed away. "I don't need this crap", he said to himself. "Who are these guys? And what do they want with me?" He didn't want to worry Sara and after all it was Sunday Morning, his and Sara's time. Matt tried to push it out of his mind. When he entered the living room, Sara was waiting. She had prepared breakfast and put the silver tray on the coffee table. He flashed a smile of approval and they settled into their usual positions on the sofa.

A few minutes later Sara looked up from her reading. "I think that they are really gonna go though with it Matt." "Who is going through with what?" He asked. "Listen to this." Sara began to read. "The spokes person for operation HOPE held a press conference to announce the purchase of 12 retired cruise ships that will be cut into sections and transported to the Pocono's, Adirondacks, and Catskill Mountain region before being reassembled and retro fitted in preparation for the new underground communities. Each location will consist of three ships buried twenty feet beneath the surface in the shape of a triangle to allow easy access from one ship to another. Each ship will operate as a self-contained underground city housing nine thousand adults and children for a combined total of twenty-seven thousand people upon completion. According to Zackary, the groups' representative areas such as the indoor pools, discos, and casinos will be converted into living quarters or vegetable gardens to supplement our food supply. The first of these underground cities will be built in the Anirondacks. It will be called Sanctuary. When asked why all three locations selected were in the Mountain regions Zackary replied. "Based on the information available to us at this time there is an eighty per cent probability that the impact of the colliding planet will be in the Atlantic Ocean. This would cause major flooding. Our scientists feel that these locations would best protect these brave American citizens from floods, fire, or a nuclear winter. Whatever the outcome we will be prepared."

"Thus far, the group has raised a whopping 80 million dollars and is assisting groups in other countries in implementing similar plans. Those who oppose the under ground cities have called the plan fool hearty or suicidal and have begun to refer to the group as the Bottom Dwellers." Sara looked up and realized that Matt's attention had drifted elsewhere. "Matthew Matteo you haven't heard a word I said." Sara tried to console him. "You can't blame yourself for Dave's death. It was carbon monoxide poisoning from a faulty cabin heater." There was no way that you could have prevented it. Sara was only half-right. Matt was not responsible for Dave's death but she was wrong in assuming that Matt was thinking of Dave. Matt could not stop thinking about the men in the GTO. That horrible feeling that he had on the day after Sara was attacked was back. The cloud of doom that hung over everyone's heads all winter seemed to lift just a bit with the arrival of spring.

The cherry blossoms were in full bloom. It was a picture perfect Thursday afternoon in the park. Julie and Art fed the beautiful white swans as they gracefully glided up to catch an afternoon snack. The tranquil scene was disrupted when two secret service men approach the happy couple. "Good afternoon Mr.

Collins, Miss. The President would like to see you now." He motioned toward the black Sedan with the tinted glass windows. As Art approached the car, he could barely make out the figure in the back seat. "Hello Art, good to see you again Julie." It was Will. "Before you say anything I know as much about this as you."

The agents dropped Julie off on the way to the White House. Art and Will huddled in the back seat whispering to one another trying to figure out what was going on. Meanwhile eight men and women sat grim faced around a large mahogany table waiting for Art and Will to arrive. Most of them had become familiar to Art and Will. CIA, Homeland Security, FBI, and the Vice President were there when they entered the room. "Have a seat, gentlemen. The President is on his way down." Just then, President Walker walked in a carrying a copy of Matt's and Will's last book. "I will get right to the point," he said still holding the book.

"Several of the world's leaders are still not convinced of the impeding danger to our planet. If they are not convinced that they are in danger, more than two billion people will die a painful, horrible death. It has been so busy since we have announced our evacuation plans that I barely have had time to go to the John. I will be meeting with these leaders here at the White House in less than two hours and I am no closer to convincing them that I was a month ago. He turned toward Will and Art. You boys have been holding out on me. He pointed the book in the direction of the two men. An hour ago I was handed this book by my secretary." He dropped the book on the table. The thud was so loud that everyone jumped in their seats. "Just who in the hell is Mathew Matteo and why wasn't I told about him?" All eyes were on Art and Will. They knew that they could no longer protect Matt. Will decided to speak up. "Mr. President. Matt was my partner. Several months ago his wife was attacked and..." "Where is he now?" The President snapped. "There are lives at stake, man! There may be something that he could tell us that you two may have overlooked." Art finally found his voice. "Well sir, he should be leaving the office about now. He works at America's Pulse." The director of Homeland Security could hardly believe his ears. "Did you say America's Pulse?" "Yes", he replied. The director looked at the men and women around the table. He chose his words very carefully. "Mr. President, I believe we have a situation here." "Yes", I agree said the FBI director. "You see that fella Dave that was murdered up at his cabin about a week ago. Well, he was the guy who took those pictures of the alien space ship that was splashed across the newspapers. He also worked at America's Pulse."

"Wait just a minute", said Will, "According to the papers Dave's death was an accident, carbon monoxide poisoning." The CIA director tossed a file across the table to the President. "Poisoned yes, accident….. that's what we told the press. In the interest of National Security, we felt that it was best not to tip our hand until we knew who and why this man was murdered. We found cigarette butts and shoe prints that didn't match any brand sold here in the United States. The cabins heating system didn't malfunction; it was deliberately altered so that the gas would leak. After Dave outlived his usefulness, they simply turned on the gas after they hit him over the head to knock him out. That probably means that they are coming for your friend next." Will called Matt on his cell phone. "Matt, it's Will, where are you?" "Hey buddy. What's up?" Matt's tone was too light-hearted, he didn't know the situation at hand. Will repeated the question, "Where are you right now?" "I am about five minutes from home." He paused. "Why?" "I think you're in danger." Matt looked through his rear view mirror. "Crap! Two guys are following me, been following me for a couple of days now. What do they want?" "I am not sure but I think they killed that guy you worked with. Listen, Matt. Go home and lock the doors. I will be right there."

Will hung up and turned to President Walker. "Two men are following Matt. I am going……." "Wait a minute." The President blocked Will's path holding up his hand. He turned to the director of Homeland Security. "Send a few agents with him. I want those jokers picked up and I wanna see Mr. Matteo in my office pronto. It's time he got with the program, now Go!"

The men in the black GTO were taken in without a struggle. Art and Will brought Matt up to speed while the agents waited outside. Will's tome was somber. "Sorry man but we had no choice. It all makes sense now. Somehow, Dave must have followed us; and took those pictures of the ship. My guess is that they wanted to see him to find out about the aliens. But, why did they kill him? And why were they following you?" Sara was listening from the top of the stairs. "Thanks for the heads up guys but I am not going with you." Matt remained defiant. "My place is here." "It's clear to me that your co-worker Dave fingered you as the alien contact. Maybe they are hoping that you will lead them to the ship or something. What if they send more guys? What if they get tired of waiting? You know what they are capable of and besides without your knowledge we will never get the ships built in time. You are the only one that can save us all."

Sara came down the stairs and gave Matt a long hug. "How much did you hear?" said Matt. "I don't know what you have to do with this Alien stuff but I heard enough to know that Will and Art are right. And I think that in your heart you know it too." Matt stared into Sara's eyes. He took a deep breath and let it out slowly. Matt turned to Will. "The odds are against you dude. Three to one come on Matt. We need you. Hell, the world needs you" Matt turned back to Sara. "Okay I will help, but; I don't want to leave you here. Like Art said, "It's not safe anymore."

Matt's relationship with the President got off on a rocky start. Like oil and water, the two didn't agree on much. "Mr. Matteo I must say that I am very disappointed in your lack of patriotism and corporation thus far." Matt smiled at President Walker. "I am afraid, Mr. President that I will continue to disappoint you if my conditions are not met." Art turned to Will. "Holy crap! Can he talk to the President like that?" Will smiled with amusement. "He just did. This is gonna be good." Matt continued. "In exchange for my help, I want round the clock protection for my wife in a secure location." The President mustered all the self-control he had. He was furious inside. No one had spoken to him like that since his childhood. "Okay Matt, we will find your wife a safe house outside the city and post a few guards, how's that?" Matt looked him straight into his eyes. "Not good enough sir. I want the same protection that you have for your wife." The President was very close to his breaking point. "That's not possible", he snapped. "That would mean secret service and they are assigned here. Are you suggesting that you and your wife move into the White House?" "Yes sir, those are my terms. And a body guard for when she need to visit. I can't think of a safer place on Earth than here." The President erupted. "Just who in the hell do you think you are? No deal!" He shouted. "Have it your way Mr. President." Matt gave a wave as he walked out the door and down the hall. Everyone in the room stood with their jaws dropped. Everyone was quiet until Will spoke up. "Ah, Mr. President, I don't think that it would be wise for you to let Matt go. You see sir, Matt is the key." The President was smoking. He was only half listening to Will. "Well, we will just get the key from him. I don't need him." Will had tried again. "Sir, you don't understand. Matt doesn't have the key, he is the key. Everything we need to know, all the missing pieces, all of the answers are in his head. Without him we are totally screwed." President Walker turned to Will. He had finally gotten his attention. "How is this possible son?" "The aliens implanted everything in his head sir." "That's crap", said the President. "Don't give me any of that sci-fi mumbo jumbo. I don't have time to play games." Everyone in the room began to whisper, until Art spoke out. "It's true, every word of it." The whispers grew louder this time. President Walker stared first at Art then at Will. He picked up the phone and said, "Do not let Mathew Matteo off the premises. Tell him, no, ask him to come back to see me." Richard Walker had been a politician for forty-two years. During that time, he had learned how to take a negative situation and turn it into something positive. He lead Matt into his private study where they could speak in private. "Well Matt, looks like we got things started off on the wrong foot. Let's try again, shall we?" "Fine by me", said Matt. "I admire your loyalty to your wife. Such loyalty is in short supply these days. I have decided to honor your request. Since you are going to be my houseguest, I have a request of my own. You don't have to like or respect me but I insist you respect the office I hold. Are we clear?" "Fair enough Mr. President." The two shook hands and rejoined the others. The Chief of Staff entered the room right after Matt and the President. "Mr. President all of the guests except the President of Russia have arrived. He is in route from the airport." "Thank you I will be up shortly." The President clapped his hands twice to get everyone's attention. "Okay folks we are just about out of time. Matt we need something to convince these stubborn jackasses that the world is in real danger and the threat is real. What can you tell us?" Matt shook his head side to side. "It doesn't work that way Mr. President. Let me explain. They called me the key but I still need the lock…something to go on. For example, if I show you a bike, car, and truck parts you would be able to separate the parts then assemble each vehicle. Do you understand? It's like word association but with pictures." Matt's eyes searched the room to see if he was getting through to anyone. "I think I get it", said Walker. The President led the group to the war room in the basement. Matt was the only one in the group who had not been there before. He was very impressed. "I sure would hate to have to pay this electric bill. Wow, so this is where my taxes are going?" A hundred or so workers mostly tech people continued with their work. Matt focused on the five jumbo screens. He grabbed his head and began to slump forward. Will rushed to his side. "What is it he asked?" "Overload", Matt replied. "There is too much information." Will yelled to the man at the master controls. "Shut down the screens! Shut down everything! Hurry!" Art brought over a chair and Matt sat down. He looked at the President. "Could you have them route everything through the center screen." "No problem". Walker began barking out orders in his gruff commanding voice. "Display all the data on the middle screen, eliminate the portions that we already understand, and then display each one slowly. Bring this man a microphone and record every word he says." Once the recorder was set up and everyone seated, Matt gave the signal to start. "First slide Easter Island, Carbomagusto once contained inside statues. Heat to 2,420 F to extract adds to one part sulphur compound while making fuel, next slide, Pyramid of the Sun, one of nineteen Astral Corridors for rescue ships to leave earth." Everyone starred in pure amazement. "Slide three, star chart of Earth's solar system indicating the exact position of each plane on the year, month and day of earth's destruction." Matt was on a roll. The President's new houseguest was earning his keep. "Next please. Stonehenge the original meeting place for first contact between humans and people from the Lazarian race. Next is the White Pyramid of China, the second of 19 astral corridors. Pyramids were constructed to hide stabilizers underground designed to keep gateways open and in place. Next please, star chart of new earth's solar system. Travel time is nine months six hours and thirty three minutes." "Unbelievable." Walker was now sure that Matt and the others were not telling them all that they knew, but now was not the time. *I'll get to the bottom of this later* he thought to himself. The assistant to the President whispered into his ear. "Sir, they are waiting for you upstairs." Time had run out. The President motioned for the man running the control board to come over. The screen went dark and the slim balding man got up from the chair and approached the President. "Yes, sir." "Bob can you set up a computer link from here to the meeting room upstairs and if you can how long will it take?" "Yes, Mr. President no problem we can have a laptop up and running in ten minutes." "Great! Thanks Bob." President Walker had not given up hope. Walker smiled and squeezed Bob's shoulder. He turned to the staff to give final instructions. "Okay everyone, listen up. Keep working your way through the material. When you find anything that we can use to sway, the undecided nations forward it to the computer upstairs. Bob will you fill you in, Mrs. Robinson you're with me. I need you to monitor the screen. I want you sitting next to me. The moment you have something let me know."

Thirty minutes into the meeting, Richard Walker's luck began to change. Mrs. Robinson tapped him gently on his shoulder. "Rich", she whispered as she nodded toward the screen. There was a picture of the Sphinx, and a caption at the bottom, that read: We have found something important. "Mrs. Robinson please have Mr. Matteo join us."

The leaders took a short break to allow the technicians to set up a view screen for Matt. Matt used the break to fill the President and Mrs. Walker in on what he had found. When the meeting reconvened, Matt was given the floor. After walking everyone through the various images shown earlier to the team in the basement he put up the familiar images of the Sphinx. "Ladies and gentlemen exactly four hundred meters beneath the base of the Sphinx is a box containing a diagram and instruction on how to construct a probe that will travel to this solar system and send back photos of the new Earth. A freshly interrupted document tells us that the probe can be constructed and launched. It'll reach it's destination as little as ninety days."

The Russian Ambassador was very skeptical. "Lies." He blurted out. "Fabrications." "Our scientist have determined that his so called New Earth is at least eight times further away than the planet Mars. A satellite takes years to make the trip." Matt stared at the ambassador. He did not like being called a liar. "Sir." Matt responded in a condescending tone. "This is not Aeroflot Airlines, nor is it an ordinary satellite. The probe will be made from the same materials used to construct the new space ships that will make it lighter and faster. It'll use only one tenth the fuels because it will be launched into what the aliens refer to as the "Flash Lanes" a type of space super highway miles above the earth over pyramids including portals above China, Egypt, and Mexico. This technology is like nothing we have ever seen." President Walker ended the meeting by promising to send the updated information to each of the representatives. Little did they know that the information he promised did not come from any chart of crop circles but from the mind of Matt Matteo.

It was almost one year to the day last August when Will and Matt discovered the last crop circle in the wheat field. Since then the whole world changed dramatically. Will, Art, Matt and the President waited at the control center in the belly of the White House along with forty or so members of the Earth Two teams and a few politicians. The President looked at Matt and smiled. "Matt, you have really come through for us. I have to admit that at first I had my doubts about you. I was sure you were a fraud. Your knowledge and work along with Art and Will have put us ahead of schedule. Hell, you've even convinced the remaining countries to prepare their people for evacuation." "Thanks Mr. President but we aren't out of the woods yet. I understand that you cast your vote to allow the Chinese, Japanese, and Russians to build and launch the probe in order to convince them of the danger and get them on board, but what if they botch it. Suppose we don't get pictures from the new solar system?" Art was sitting to Matt's right listening to the conversation. "Excuse me gentlemen but we sill have the problem of the North Koreans." "Yes", Walker nodded, the only holdout. "Those North Koreans are stubborn as hell. My people in Homeland Security tell me that foreigners and computer hackers are charging as much as one hundred grand for fake US citizenship papers. They are afraid they won't get out if they stay in any of the countries that got a later start." "But the Koreans" he paused and shook his head slowly. "I am afraid they are totally screwed." The Vice President stepped off the elevator and joined the others. "Well this is it images should be coming through in about four minutes." The Vice President pulled up a chair. Everyone stared quietly at the big screens as if they were waiting for a movie to begin.

A few minutes passed and Will glanced down at his Rolex. "It should be any second now." The center screen began to flicker. Bob made a few adjustments and there it was. There were twelve crystal clear images of planets that formed a solar system with not one but two moons next to the blue planet. Art gave a low whistle. "Holy Cow! It's beautiful." "Magnificent" said Matt. The room suddenly broke out in spontaneous applause. The President picked up the mike. "Ladies and gentlemen, well done. We are on our way." Screens 2 and 3 began to flicker. Pictures of Earth 2 came into focus. The technician was working his magic. Bringing up screens four and five he shouted. The screens were a wash of colors and endless streams of pictures began to come through. There could no longer be any doubt New Earth did indeed exist.

Summer seemed to pass quickly. Thanksgiving was just around the corner. Art, Will, and Matt were working fourteen hour days since August. Sunday morning was Sara's favorite time of the week. Being a resident of the White House has its advantages but it also has a few drawbacks, like not being able to have a New Year's Party or having lunch with girlfriends. Walker had made good on his word to give her protection. He came in the form of a six foot two Samoan bodyguard. Vai was Sara's new shadow. Whenever she left the Whitehouse he was never more than a few feet away. Vai was strong, smart and kind. Sara knew that she was safe when he was around but felt uncomfortable socializing with her girlfriends with a bodyguard towering over her. Sara pondered these things as she peered out of the window watching the workers assemble the spacecraft parts on the White House lawn. She didn't notice that Matt had returned with a hefty stack of Sunday papers from a half dozen countries. He put the papers down and held her from behind with his arms around her waist. "I didn't think that it was going to be so big", said Sara. "I mean look at it—it's huge." "I just hope it flies." said Matt. "I brought the papers up. You ready babe?" "Yeah", she nodded "I guess. We both know what they are going to say. It's all anyone talks about anymore. Let's see." Sara searched through the stack and began reading aloud. "Moscow, Russians scrambled to make up for lost time, scientist and technicians work round the clock to complete first two ships in Red Square and Pushkin Square by years end. Mexico, President Foxx gave local leaders the grand tour of the Space Vessel located on the Zocalo in Mexico City. China, The People's Republic of China has announced the construction of ships four, five and six will begin Thursday at Tiananmen Square." "Okay Sara. I think you've made your point." "No! No!" Sara held up her hand. "There's more. London England protesters angered over royal family's decision to exclude commoners from traveling on the Royals Ship. The Prime Minister is to meet with the Queen later today. Additional ships are under contruction at Hyde Park and Victoria Park. Okay, I'm done, unless you want to hear the Canadian news." "Sara don't forget what the doctor said. If you don't bring your stress level down you may not get pregnant again." "Matt, I'm bored. You work with your two best friends everyday and play Pinochle with the Vice President every Friday night. I can't go out can't even cook anymore and to top things off I can't tell my friends everything that's going on. How am I supposed to relieve the stress?" Matt's eyes shifted towards the bedroom. "Oh, stop it Matt. I am serious. The only female that I can talk to is Julie and she spends most of her time with Art when she is in town." "Okay Sara. I'm sorry." Sara walked over to the window to look at the ship again. She smiled at Matt, then turned back to the window. "I've been going about this the wrong way. Everyone's so obsessed with these damn ships and I have been fighting it. Instead, I should be helping. She smiled and pointed out the window. I want to help. Matt, get me a job working on that ship." "Doing what?" Matt asked. "I don't care what. I just need to be a part of something useful instead of sitting around on my butt all day."

CHAPTER 10

▼

TROUBLE IN RIVER CITY

President Walker gave his State of the Union address from the bridge of the recently completed Spacecraft One. "My fellow Americans, I am speaking to you from one of the seventeen completed spacecrafts in our great country. Within the next six month's the dedicated men and women who helped to build this fine aircraft will be completing work on three more ships located in Central Park, New York. Another four in the desert outside of Las Vegas, five at The Bonneville Salt Flats in Utah, two in Fairmount Park in Philadelphia, and five in Dallas, Ft. Worth area in Texas. The news of the impending destruction of Earth has caused peace to break out in the four corners of the world. In the past year, ninety percent of our troops abroad have returned home. The divorce rate here at home has dropped significantly while the birth rate has increased dramatically. All of this is great news, but it comes at a hefty price. The numbers of space vessels needed for evacuating our citizens have been revised upward. In order to reach out minimum number of ships in time I have instructed the Joint Chiefs of Staff to redeploy all available military personnel to aid in the construction of the escape ships nearest to his or her base. No new applications for citizenship will be accepted until we reach our new home planet, and finally I am requesting that all couples refrain from starting a family or expanding their family until we reach Earth 2. It is our pledge to leave no American behind."

While the President continued to speak. Will, Art, Matt, Mrs. Robinson and members of the space project were watching from the monitors in the ships community center twenty floors below. Sara arrived a few minutes after Walker's speech but before the President and Vice President. Since appointed as the Director of hydroponics Development or DHD for short, she has been keeping busy. The President thanked everyone for coming. "I will get right to the point. I am concerned that with the current rate of growth in our population we just will not have enough ships to transport everyone. The murder rate has dropped and a significant number of bottom dwellers have come to their senses. Boys and girls, we have a problem here. I have asked you all here to come up with some answers. We only have six years to…" One of the junior aides burst into the room. "Mr. President! Mr. President! Sorry sir, but I think that you will want to see this." Without waiting for the President to respond, he turned on all the monitors for CNN, FOX, MSNBC, and the BBC. "From California to Boston people, mostly men have taken to the streets." "Turn it up" the President ordered. "Calm down son, yes that's right" said the reporter. "Several hundred local residents who live nearby one for the new space ship construction sites have decided to pitch in. I have never seen anything like it. Some are even carrying toolboxes and work gloves. Right now, they are forming a caravan of pickup trucks, cars, and even a flat bed truck is being used to transport these patriotic souls to the work site. I'll turn it back over to you in the studio." "Turn up CNN." The aide adjusted the volume. A woman clutching a microphone tried desperately to keep pace with the men and women in the crowded streets. "Not since nine eleven have I seen such an outpouring of unity. People of every, age, race, color, and gender are uniting for a common cause. Right now, I am in the center of about two hundred or so people walking down Main Street. We are about three blocks from the entrance to the construction site. Okay. If you look over my left shoulder, you can make out the dome or top of one of three ships undergoing construction in this area. As I look around this crowd, I see men, women and yes, children carrying power tools, toolboxes, and even a few hammers. One man is even carrying a flag of The United Stats. I guess after what has been reported about citizens from other countries being left behind these folks aren't taking any chances." Shut it off, said Eric. The Vice President turned to the President. "Now what?" asked Mrs. Robinson. "Call legal. Have them draft the necessary forms to protect the government form any lawsuits. Fax them to all the sights with a memo then get General Leslie on the phone for me. We are going to need more security on and around these ships." "Yes sir, she replied before leaving the room." The President looked relieved. "Ladies and gentlemen, problem solved." Meeting adjourned.

Art and Will were invited to Sara and Matt's for drinks. Will had that look in his eyes and Matt knew what it meant. When Matt was in earshot Will whispered to him. "Man, having hundreds of strangers roaming round those ships ain't cool." "I hear ya," said Matt. Sara served the guys drinks and the four sat dumbfounded as they tried to understand how The President could not see the potential danger in allowing hundreds of people to roam freely on the growing fleet of ships.

One year and one hundred and four ships later things were looking up. With all the additional workers more parts plants were constructed. Soon they would be able to complete a ship a day but things were not going as well in other parts of the world.

Will was a sound sleeper, but his houseguest was not. He continued to snore when Theresa got out of bed late one night. The flashing green light from under the closet door drew her across the bedroom floor like a moth to the flame. It was the night before the full moon and not one of the three men noticed the Celestial event. The aliens had returned and were summoning Will, Art and Matt for a meeting. Theresa reached for the handle on the door and was about to discover the alien receiver tucked away under Will's shoeboxes inside the closet when the phone rang. "Hello", Will said into the phone without realizing that the other side of the bed was unoccupied. "Will, it's Art. Check your receiver." Will rubbed his eyes "What?" "They're back!" Art shouted. "The aliens are back!" Will sprang from the bed and ran across the room just as Theresa pulled the closet door open. Will slammed the door as hard as he could. "What in the hell's your problem?" Theresa snapped. "You damn near took my fingers off. Will you have been acting very strange lately. First, you disappear for months without one single phone call and no reasonable explanation and now this! What's in there?" Will was clearly stalling until he could come up with a good explanation. "Huh? I mean, well. Oh just a minute I gotta take this call. Come back to bed and I will explain everything." He had no idea how to get out of this one. "Hey, Art are you still there?" "Yes, Will. Tell her it's a surprise gift. Say it's broken and you have to replace it. Meet me at Matt's tomorrow okay." "Thanks man, I owe you." Will smiled and hung up the phone as he turned to an angry Theresa. Will was not accustomed to lying but in this case, he made an exception. The story worked because Theresa's birthday was only a few weeks away so all was forgiven by morning.

Matt, Will and Art huddled over morning coffee and a box of Crispy Cream Doughnuts while Sara made her way to the hydroponics lab aboard the ship. Will sipped his coffee and glared at Matt from across the table. "Matt, you can't be serious. There is no way that you can go with us and not be missed." "I have to agree with Will," said Art. "How will you explain your absence to the Vice President at tomorrow night's card game?" Will tapped his index finger on the calendar on the table. "February 2, 2007 is the night of the full moon. We all knew that someday they could come back. Something tells me that the news is not going to be good." "Guys! Matt pointed to his head. You're not the ones having the strange dreams. I need to know what's going on up here. I will talk to Eric. The Vice President is pretty cool once you get to know him. I won't tell him where I am going. I will just ask him to cover for me don't worry."

Later that day Matt saw his chance. After he made his pitch, Eric turned to him. "I thought we were friends." Matt seemed a bit confused. "We are friends." "So, stop trying to BS me Matt. I know you're not sick, and the reason why you are not playing Pinochle with us tonight probably has something to do with your partners in crime Art, Will and your alien buddies. Look, whatever you say stays in this room. I think you know me well enough to know that I am a man of my word. If it weren't for you and your friends, we would be up the creek by now. Go wherever you have to go tonight and do what you have to do. If you need anything from me just let me know." Matt was surprised he had found a true ally in the Vice President.. The second most powerful man in the country if not the world had just given him his unconditional support. Matt didn't know quite how to respond. He decided on humor. "You know I could use a private plane tonight." They both laughed. Then Eric looked directly at Matt and said, "Would a helicopter do? It's the best I could do on such sort notice." "You're kidding right? No said the Vice President I am very serious. The chopper is yours for the night. No flight plan will be filled and there are no markings on the craft." Eric sat on the edge of his desk and started dialing the phone. "I hope you like black." Matt went from extreme gratitude to pure amazement. "You got to be joking, Black Helicopters?" "That's right," said Eric. "But if you tell anyone then I would have to have you shot. It's a joke Matt. Lighten up will ya." After Eric made the call, he patted Matt on the back as they walked to the door. "Let's grab some lunch my friend"

Art, Matt, and Will landed on a private airstrip in an isolated area outside of North Salem, New Hampshire. There was a car waiting to take them into town where they picked up a rental. Before heading to Stonehenge, US, they drove around to see if they were being followed. "Well, all clear," said Art. "We should stop for petro before we leave" "Ditto," said Matt, "let's go."

The ship landed earlier than normal but that was not all that was different. "This was not the same ship." "Guys," Will was leery "What's up? This ship is four times the size of T'zar's ship. What did they do trade up?" Will got his answer when the door opened. Two attractive females appeared at the ships entrance, "Come quickly, please hurry." The women appeared to be in their thirties. Both had long platinum hair one cropped the others long and flowing down her back. One of the women was a little shorter. Oddly enough, both women had hazel eyes. They beckoned the men to move faster so that they could cloak the large ship. Matt looked disappointed. "Where are Onan and T'zar?" The taller of the two women answered. "I bid you peace. "I am Nyssa and this is Lysta. Our leaders from the Earth's Guardians sends their warm greetings along with regrets from the two of whom you speak. Lysta and I were sent because Onan and T'zar are under the watchful eye our government. It was too risky for them after their last journey here. We bring you important news." Will shook his head. "Here it comes," Lysta gestured to the seats "Please, be seated." "These are for you." Art handed Nyssa a box of Godiva Chocolates. "It's chocolate candy." "Ah, yes, Nyssa smiled as she accepted the gold box. My life mate T'zar shared chocolate with us that he received from you after his visits. Thank you. He will be pleased." Matt was curious about Nyssa's comment about T'zar. "Did I hear you say that you and T'zar are married?" "That is correct," she replied. "Lysta and Onan are joined as well. Everyone believes that we are visiting friends on a distant planet. Your rescue has been hampered by one or two members on the council alliance who voted against saving Earth. We intercepted a message from our home world sent to the Otarians based here on Earth." A top secret schematic detailing highly classified information on the ships structure and computer systems was passed on during a recent transmission. Since it is forbidden for the Otarians to openly attack any race including humans the leader of our alliance is certain that the people of Otar have or will soon recruit your people to do their bidding.

Thanks for the warning said Matt, but you said that the Otarians are on Earth now. I think that their ships would be pretty hard to miss. Not really Lysta replied. Otarians have become very skilled at pulling the sheep over your eyes. Nyssa laughed. Ah Lysta that's wool, wool over ones eyes. For centuries humans have been duped into believing that all UFO's came from outer space when in fact Otarians have maintained two bases under the sea here on Earth for some time now. Only one is still operational, the other located near Gulf Breeze is no longer in use. Everything is now run from The Eye of Neptune or Neptune's Eye for short.

Observe. With a wave of her hand the lights on the ship went dim. Lysta then operated a series of buttons located in the panel on the chairs armrest. All of the seats began to recline the familiar blue globe appeared on the ceiling. Earth's image was instantly recognizable. While Nyssa began the briefing Nyssa kept watch of the small monitor placed in front of her. Before Lysta could get pass the second sentence Lysta called out to Nyssa. "Check the monitor!" she yelled. I see it Lysta. Get us out of here! Now!

Lysta rushed over to the pilots chair and seconds later the ship began to rise. What's happening? said a worried looking Art. Two Otarian patrol ships, explained Nyssa. They are heading this way from the west. Better make that three yelled Lysta. I cannot tell what class ships they are from this range but if we are lucky they won't get here for a few more minutes. However if they are flying the newer models..... Nyssa paused, well it may already be to late. If they have detected us then we will be pursued.

Will sprang from his seat and turned to Lysta. What are you waiting for?

"We have to go!" Will said. "Go!" repeated Lysta mocking Will's tone. "We have already gone", she said proudly. "Are current position is over the Atlantic Ocean. To be precise we are hovering exactly thirty-seven and one half kilometers above it." Nyssa smiled at Will. "You are aboard the Silver Unicorn: one of the fastest ships in the entire galaxy. In our world, we name our vessels after men or animals who have exhibited great speed, strength and agility. The Unicorn has an abundance of these and more." Lysta held the monitor with both hands. "Here they come. Shutting down all non-essential power," she whispered. "Everyone please be silent. G class," she whispered softly to herself. A minute or two later the ship seemed to come alive again. Everything was restored to normal. "The patrol has passed under us," she announced with a sigh of relief. "That was awfully close." "Too close," said Nyssa. "We will be safe as long as we remain here. Let us continue. When we have concluded our business, perhaps you will take food with us."

Once again Will, Art and Matt were sitting in the reclined position watching the screen change from Earth, to the California coastline then to the Philippines. With one hand on the controls embedded into the armchair Nyssa used her free hand to point to the ocean on the screen above. "We have been monitoring this area around the clock. Neptune's Eye is located on the ocean's floor almost seven miles from the surface. We are certain that this location was selected for it's privacy. The location off the Florida coast that was referred to as Poseidon was abandoned due to the increase of ship traffic in recent years. As I stated before the interruption Neptune's Eye base is, an observation post, if you will. The Otarians we encountered earlier most likely came from that base. When humans discovered the Marina's Trench the base was already operational. Selecting the deepest darkest area was probably the smartest decision they had ever made." The suspense was killing Matt. He finally blurted his question. "How do they get down there? Where are their subs kept?" Lysta and Nyssa tried to contain their laughter. "Please excuse our bad manners. There is and always has been a misconception or myth that air ships or UFO's were only ment to fly when, in point of fact, space ships began as what you call submarines. Very few humans have ever seen a submerged space vessel." "Yes, of course," said Art. "I recall reading something about an incident in the sixties I believe. A UFO was tracked by the town's people for days in a place called Shag Harbor, I believe it was in Canada. It traveled underwater and after a few days, it just took off." "That is correct Art," said Nyssa. "Nova Scotia 1967. All members of our organization must study these events before we are allowed to travel to your world. The Otarians have simply exploited your lack of knowledge about space vessels. While everyone is looking up, they are traveling under the sea. Shall we continue? You three must discover what nefarious plan will be hatched by using the ships diagrams as your focus. Perhaps the motive is sabotage. The Otarians will stop at nothing to take possession of your new home planet. In the event that the first plot fails, rest assured that they have a back up plan. I regret to inform you that due to sunspots, meteor showers and solar flares, we were only able to intercept the bare minimum of facts. Keeping in mind that these are a bold and brazen group, they are preparing to send a delegation to Earth to meet with your world leaders. We have surmised that they will impersonate our Supreme Leader in an attempt to keep you from leaving earth. Our government would never do such a thing." "Yes, Will. What is it?" "Sorry to interrupt, but when is this going to happen? And how are we supposed to tell our President that these guys are bogus if we aren't supposed to have this info?" Everyone in the room was silent. Now they fully understood why the aliens had come back. "I cannot say", said Nyssa. "You must resolve this issue among yourselves. You have been warned. You must not speak of any of this to your people." Suddenly Matt's issues with his dreams seemed insignificant. What the heck? He though. It wouldn't hurt to ask. The two women were unable to offer any help to Matt. All they could offer was sympathy and a promise to pass the message to T'zar when they returned home.

The men were given a quick tour of the ship before being led into the dinning area. The food looked and smelled delicious. Matt reached to sample the goods. He held up what appeared to be a piece of fruit shaped like a banana but orange in color. Lysta tapped Matt on the hand. "Before we take food, we must first pray reverence to Yeshua. You know him as the Christ. When we give thanks to Yeshua we honor the creator as well." After the food was blessed, Nyssa described each dish that the women had prepared. No attention was paid to the music playing in the background until Matt began humming the tune. Everyone starred at Matt in absolute amazement. Nyssa even dropped her fork. "That's impossible," she claimed. Still unaware of what he had just done Matt looked at Nyssa. "What's impossible?" "That song," she said. "It was just released two weeks before our trip from our home world." T'zar uploaded it into our database right before we made our departed. "He's been singing it since it was recorded. But it's only been out a short time. You not only have his past knowledge your mind must still be linked somehow. That's amazing. Nothing like this has ever happened before." At that moment, Nyssa and Lysta's eyes changed from hazel to a lime green. Will, Art, and Matt noticed the change instantly. Will jumped from his seat. "What the? What's with the eyes?" Lysta tried to calm the guys down. "Please don't be alarmed. You have much to learn about us. Allow me to explain. Humans express themselves through words, hand movements, and facial expressions. Our ancestors realized that it is quite easy to deceive with words or expressions but not with the eyes. One of your great writers once said that, "the eyes are the window to the soul." Our pupils have been genetically augmented to react to seventeen emotions and feelings by changing color. In a few moments it will pass." Art moved closer to Lysta. He started directly into her eyes. "Interesting, it's a bloody built in lie detector." "Oh, it's much more than that," said Nyssa. The eyes can detect pain, sadness, pleasure, joy, surprise, illness and more. Some of our people have learned to control the colors by thought. "Yes, yes," Matt said. "It's like beating a lie detector. But wait, when we met with Onan and T'zar why didn't their eyes change? The women looked at one another but were hesitant to respond. Nyssa continued reluctantly with her explanation. "The males in our world undergo a medical procedure when they reach the age of accountability. They are given what is known as blockers. I believe you call them contact lenses. Any female who undergoes this process is perceived as having something to hide. As you can see, even an advanced society such as ours is not without social problems and double standards. Still, we do not blame our mates. It has been and still is our way, at least for now," she added.

The dinner party lasted almost three hours everyone had lots of questions. *It was a good meeting* thought Will. When they landed Matt's cell phone rang. It was Eric. "Matt, Eric, we've got a problem. A couple of hours ago SETI reported three ships headed toward the Atlantic coast. I have been trying to reach you. The President is climbing the walls. He thinks that you know more than what you are telling him and he thinks that Sara and I are covering for you but he can't prove it. You need to get back here pronto. By the way, he can't locate Will or Art either. Do you know where they are? On second thought, don't answer that. I don't want to know." "Okay, Eric." Matt cupped the phone to prevent the others from listening. Matt was always quick on his feet. "I need to have a rental car picked up." Nyssa and Lysta dropped the trio off right on the White House lawn behind the massive Space Force 1 so that no one could see. Since Nyssa cloaked the ship SETI could detect their arrival The two women waved goodbye and Art, Will, and Matt crept aboard the ship unseen.

The men held a strategy session in the community room in the upper level of the ship. "So we were here all evening, right?" He looked at Art then Will they nodded in agreement. "Okay, here we go." Matt dialed the President's office. "Good Evening, Mrs. Robinson you sure are working late tonight." "Is this Matt?" She said. "Yes, Ma'am." "I don't know where you and your partners have been all night but I hope that you are wearing your asbestos underwear cause the President is breathing fire right now. Where are you?" "I am on the ship outside," he replied. "Hold on. I will put you through." It didn't take long for President Walker to find Matt on the ship. He and the Vice President sat on one side of the table while the guys sat opposite them. "You expect me to believe that you three were here all night and don't know anything whatsoever about the sightings tonight?" "What sightings?" Will said with all the innocence that he could muster. "Oh don't give me that crap!" The President yelled. "There were ships up in New England four hours ago!" Now it was Matt's turn to play dumb. "Mister President if we were in New England just four hours ago how could we be here? And how did we get pass security at the front gate?" President Walker thought for a moment while Eric buried his face into his hands. The President could not answer the question so he shifted the subject. "You are trying my patience boys. If you weren't with the aliens then exactly what have you three been doing all night?" Art finally got into the debate. "Well sir. We are checking sir, checking for sabotage." The President looked as though he was about to go into cardiac arrest. "What BS are you trying to spin now?" "Sabotage! By whom? Why?" "Well sir," Art continued, "We have reason to believe that several ships have been tampered with to prevent them from flying. I, we are not at liberty to reveal our sources." The Vice President crossed his legs and turned away. He knew what was coming. "Not at liberty," Walker laughed as he repeated. In a calm voice "You guys are not the Rat Pack." His voice grew louder. "And I am not some ignorant smuck who just crawled out of the turnip patch." The President's voice grew to a roar as he rose from his seat. "You three had better damn well tell me everything you know right this second or I will have you all locked up for the rest of your natural lives." Art was really, afraid. The President was so steaming mad that he was turning red. Will turned to Matt and whispered, "Been there done that."

This was not the first time that Matt and the President had gone a few rounds. Matt tried the diplomatic approach. "Look, sir. We are trying to protect you. The less you know the less likely it is for you to blurt out something in a meeting with other leaders or God forbid the press. All it takes is one slip up and we are all doomed. We can tell you what we know but we can't tell you how we know it. Or you can lock us up and in four years, it won't matter because we will all be fried, boiled, or drowned either way we will all be dead." Eric called the President over the corner of the room. "Sir, sabotage is serious stuff. If there is just the slightest possibility that their information is correct we can't pass this up." The President stroked his chin as he looked down to the floor. He popped his head up like awaking from a trance. "Okay Eric. You seem to have a rapport with these men from now on you handle them. Find out what they know give them what they need and keep me informed." "But, Mr. President…" President Walker turned around and left the ship without speaking another word. He knew that Matt was right but he would never give him the satisfaction of telling him so.

CHAPTER 11

▼

CONSPIRACY

Will was in a foul mood. It was Saturday morning and it was raining again. Art turned on to K Street and glanced over at his grouchy passenger. He was driving them to meet Eric and Matt. Will grew more irritated as he listened to the reporter on the radio. "Thank you for joining us on this rainy Saturday morning. Today is May 10th, 2008. Don't forget to wear your water wings if you're going out today. It is eight o'clock here in soggy D.C." Will had enough and shut the radio off. "I hate the rain," Will grumbled. "It has been eight friggin straight days of rain, rain, and more rain. Why are we working on a Saturday again?" Art glanced at Will then turned back to watch the road. "Well, Will, if all goes well this may be the last time we have to deal with this problem. We have enough to put these whackos out of business for good. And besides the weatherman is predicting a sunny day for tomorrow."

Coffee, tea, and the usual assortment of pastries were laid out on the table when they arrived. Matt and Eric were already starting on their second cup of coffee. "Good Morning, gentlemen." The Vice President seemed a big more chipper than usual. "Let's get started. It looks as if the Japanese are running out of level terrain to build their ships. The locations at Ueno Park and Aso-Kuju National are at capaticy and the Queens Park location in Trinidad just caught a sabatour last night. Well enough about their problems I hope that you guys have good news for me." Art looked up from his notes. "I believe we do sir. Well, let me start by saying that Matt and Will have drafted me as the spokespersons for this meeting. As you know each space vessel is equipped with a countdown clock and according to the instructions, we will not be permitted to fire up the engines until the clocks reach zero on December of 2012. This has given the saboteurs the upper hand. We assume that our alien donors are concerned that we may go off exploring the galaxy if we could fly the ships in advance of our evacuation. Anyway, our original focus was on the folks from the underground. Humans Opposed to the Planets Evacuation or HOPE for short. If I were the Otarians that is who I would enlist to help cripple the ships since they have made it clear that they are staying and have been trying to convince others to do the same? They make up about eighty-five percent of the bottom dwellers community. You know, the ones building the under ground cities with the cruise ships for shelters. Okay, here's the thing. There is a splinter group, that is much smaller but far more radical. They call themselves the Pure Patriots. You see HOPE bases their stance on the hidden messages in the Bible. Years ago, some bloke used this code and came up with 2012 as the year of Earth's destruction, but the religious community is divided on what it means. One side says that Christians who leave Earth will miss the Second Coming, but others think that the code is the sign to leave this Earth because the good book says that God will rebuild Earth. They believe that Earth 2 was prophesized." The Vice President interrupted. "Excuse me Art. This is a fascinating Bible lesson, but what does this have to do with the ships being tampered with?"

"I was just getting to that, sir. Most Christians believe that God never intended for us to leave this Earth and that these true believers will be protected and sustained. The vast majority of these blokes are peace loving and harmless. But the Pure Patriots are a different story, these guys are real zealots. Their motivation is purely selfish. They believe that America will become a third world country if they allow the engineers, doctors, scientists, farmers, and tech heads to leave. Their goal is to prevent this at any cost. For months, we have had men on the inside. Our people have confirmed everything I have told you. Up until now, we have not been able to identify them all."

Art turned to Will. Will passed out copies of a diagram to everyone in the room. "I am sure that you all are familiar with this by now. This ship's diagram is classified but somehow the Otarians have at least one contact on the planet of Lazon who smuggled this out. The red dot indicates the location of the gyrocompass or gyro for short. The gyro prevents the ship from tipping over in flight. Disabling it is not easy and takes time. Every saboteur carries a copy of this in order to complete the disconnect procedure because removeing it would be too obvious" Matt pointed to the paper as he spoke. Find the diagram find the rat. "You mean find the dummies," said Will. "If there is anything left to the planet it will be knocked off its axis. The weather patterns will be all screwed up. It's going be damn near impossible to grow anything. And besides, where are they going to live?" "Inside the ships." said Matt. "That's the only part of their plan that makes sense. The Pure Patriots are going to use the ships as shelter. That's why they want to disable them not destroy them." The Vice President stood from his chair. "I think we have enough, well done gentlemen. I am going to brief the President. I'm gonna recommend simultaneous raids across the country and put an end to the volunteer program for building the ships." "Amen!" Will slapped the table with his pad. "While you're at it you might want to take a look around down there, after the raids have been completed. Don't forget the other shoe hasn't dropped yet. Maybe we could pick up some useful info." Eric smiled at Will. "That's what I like about you Will. You are always two steps ahead of everyone else."

The saboteurs were rooted out in less than a month and things were going as well as could be expected. This morning like most other mornings, you could find Sara experimenting in the hydroponics garden on the ship. Once a week she gave seminars via a teleconference screen to her counterparts in ships around the country. Her conference ended early so Sara grabbed her basket of plastic spray bottles and got to work. The ships vegetable garden took up an entire level of the ship if you didn't know any better you could have sworn that you were in a trop- ical rain forest. The foliage was everywhere. There was barely a path left to walk in. "Anybody home?" Will shouted. She could hear his voice call out from behind the greenery clear across the room. "Over here Will." Will made his way through the maze of green leafy plants and gave Sara a peck on the cheek. "Girl you need to slow down. What are you working on today?" Sara smiled as she con- tinued to sprits the basil plants in front of her. "Herbs," she said with a touch of pride in her voice. "We are convinced that we can grow enough food for the nine month trip so I decided to work on herbs and spices for the ship's chefs. Try say- ing that fast five times. If all goes well by next year we can start on Herbal plants to use for *medicinal* purposes. No time to slow down. What brings you down here? I thought you and Matt were supposed to go jogging upstairs." Will held his hands out with his palms upward and hunched his shoulders. "I thought so too," he said. "He's not on the track. I thought that he was down here with you." Sara's expression turned serious. "Will, I think I know where he is. I know that there has not been much for you to do since you caught the saboteurs and I really appreciate you hanging out with him more since I am busy here and Art's away in England but," Sara put down the bottle and turned to Will. "Matt's behavior has changed; I mean he's still good to me. Don't get me wrong. It's just that sometimes he seems so distant, almost melancholy. I bet that right now he's on the bridge staring at that damn countdown clock. At first I thought with the crew, the tech guys, doctors and everyone running around the ship getting ready for the big day that he was just bored but I have caught him up there at least a half dozen times just this month. Last night, after you left I finally got up enough nerve to ask him about it. He totally blew me off. Said it was nothing." Will held Sara's hand, "Look, Sara, I will have a talk with him. Don't worry. I won't mention your name. It's cool. It's going to be okay." He flashed a big smile hoping that his attempt at consoling her would help put Sara's mind at ease. "Thanks Will. I don't know what I would do without you."

The countdown clock read four years, three months and five days. Will walked up behind Matt as he stared at the glowing red numbers on the dial. Will put his hand on Matt's shoulder. "What's going on man? I thought we were supposed to go jogging. You know, knock of some of these calories from all that pizza and beer. No more crop circles to chase. We gotta work it off somehow." Matt faced Will and leaned against the console. "Will have you noticed how accepting we have all become about the destruction of our planet. I mean last night while we were watching the Olympics, we were having such a great time that for a few hours I actually forgot that the world as we know it is literally coming to an end." "Come on Matt. We play the hand that we're dealt. Life goes on. You have no reason to feel guilty…In fact, you should feel pretty damn good about yourself. If it weren't for you, billions of people would be dead in less than five years." Will pointed to the clock. "You are a hero. Accept what you cannot change." Matt looked up from the floor. "Okay Will, let's set the record straight. First, I let Sara down, and then I abandoned you and left Art swinging in the breeze. I am nobody's hero." Will had had enough. He was becoming frustrated. "Okay fine!" Will shouted as he pointed across the room. "Go sit in the corner and suck your thumb. And if you want I will pick you up a pacifier and a box of Kleenex then you can have a real pity party. Look, we all make mistakes. What's important is that you are here now, and we would not have gotten this far without you. Something's going on with you, if you don't want to tell me fine; but spare me the violins." Will waited for a response. Matt looked at Will, turned to the clock then back to Will. Will regained his composure. "Come on Matt. Talk to me man." "It's not that easy, Will. Even if I tell you, you still may not understand." "Try me." said Will. "Okay, I'll give it a shot. The problem is not me. It's T'zar. It's not just dreams anymore or music. He's going through something heavy right now and I am going through the emotions without the knowledge of knowing what the hell is going on. It scares me to think that this is somehow tied to his actions of trying to saving us. Was he caught? Is he being tortured? You see only the strong feelings seem to affect me. And lately they have been pretty intense. I know you think I am crazy." "No. No, I don't," said Will. "I think you are the bravest guy I know. Hell, I would not have done it." Will smiled and gave Matt a gentle shove. "You made the sacrifice that Art and I were not prepared to make. That took a lotta guts man. Have you talked to Sara?" Will knew he had not, but needed to nudge Matt toward telling her. "No, man I wanted to tonight but…" Will saw his opening and cut Matt off. "I think you should tell her today. I think sometimes you underestimate her. You don't have to go through this alone Matt. We will be there for you. And when Art gets back, I am sure that he will feel the same."

That evening over a candle light dinner Matt told Sara everything. Soon after the phone rang. "Matt, it's Eric. We may have a problem. Get a hold of Will and meet me in my office in twenty minutes." Shortly after the call Eric, Will and Matt were headed to the situation room in the sub-basement. Matt and Will had not been told what was happening but they knew if they were going to the nerve center of operations that it must be big. The five familiar jumbo screens were still in place but only one was on. There was a picture of the Great Wall of China. The Vice President moved swiftly around the room checking to see if everybody was in place. Bob was in his usual seat at the controls, while Mrs. Robinson was arranging documents at a desk nearby. There was another gentleman on the phone and several workers rushing about. "Okay gang", Eric clapped his hands. "Let's get this show on the road. I have a meeting with the President in ten minutes." He pointed to Bob. "Okay Bob, give us the first image please. This is an aerial shot of the baseball stadium and pavilion at the Olympics security camera. Next please. This is a view taken approximately ninety minutes ago." After what the people in the room had seen and heard over the last four years they had become somewhat jaded. They looked around the room at each other but kept silent. The picture was exactly the same as the first except everything, the entire stadium including the seats was completely covered in grass. "Bob, can you give us a close up?" Bob zoomed in. "Now there was grass where the pitchers mound was. I assure you all that this is not a hoax or a prank. This area is guarded more closely than Fort Knox. The grass literally grew over night. Botanists, Horticulturist, scientist, geologist, and every soil specialist in the world are on the way to this site as we speak." The man on the phone handed it to Eric. "Okay, I see, yes." Eric nodded as he listened to the voice on the phone. "Thank you, goodbye. Gentlemen and Mrs. Robinson, the latest image is coming through now. Bob, do you have it yet?" "Yes, sir." Bob replied. "Okay put it up." The grass had turned to a dark blue. Will leaned forward to get a closer look. "Now that's just down right impossible, when did that happen?" He asked. "Sometime between when we got off the elevator and now." said Eric. Bob switched back to the picture of the Great Wall of China. A few people were milling about. Mrs. Robinson asked if it was a live shot. "Yes, it is Mrs. Robinson." answered Bill. "Then where are all the people?" She wondered aloud. Matt smiled and whispered to Mrs. Robinson. "That's because it's six a.m. in China. They are probably just getting up."

Eric looked at his watch. "Listen up people." He started pacing as he talked. "The longer we sit here gabbing the more contaminated the site will be with people poking around. Matt, you and Will are going to investigate the site. The President and I believe that this is a result of extraterrestrial activities. Pack your gear. You leave on Marine 1 in thirty minutes. The chopper will drop you off at the military base where an F18 hornet will be waiting for you. When the President assigned me to you guys, I took the liberty of learning as much as I could about your past. If memory serves Matt you flew the F14 and F16 in the war." While Matt seemed surprised, Will was ecstatic. He leaped from his seat. "A trip to China at Uncle Sam's dime, right on! I always wanted to see the Great Wall." Matt did not share Will's enthusiasm. "Hold on a minute. I have a few questions. One, you can't fly a US Air Force Jet over China's air space without being shot down. Second, where am I supposed to land in the Forbidden City? And thirdly, why are we going in the first place?" "Fair enough," said Eric. "I will answer your last question first. I am convinced that all these so called experts aren't going to find a damn thing. You two will be the only ones there with any knowledge of aliens. Are you forgetting Matt, that you are the key? Something may click in your head. You and Will have done this hundreds of times. You have a huge advantage. As for the rest of your questions: Mrs. Robinson if you will please......" He pointed to the a plastic bag filled with documents on her desk and she handed them to Will. It was all government ID's passports, credit cards, etc. "It has all been taken care of. Land in Hawaii and board the Gulf Stream 4. The pilot of the G4 will have you in Beijing before nightfall. Have a good trip." Eric headed toward the elevator. "Get back to me as soon as you have something. Cheer up Matt. Either the ET's are trying to tell us something, or…" he entered the elevator and pressed the button before completing his sentence. "Or what?" Matt shouted. "Or you will be the first to photograph the world's largest Chia Pet." Eric laughed aloud as the elevator doors closed. You could still hear him laughing all the way up the elevator shaft. Will and Matt were chasing daylight. They refueled in California and arrived in Hawaii four and half hours after leaving Washington D.C. Matt landed the fighter jet on a private airstrip near the G4. Will admired the sleek new Gulf Stream as they walked toward the plane. "Sweet." he said to Matt. "That Eric is a man of his word. I don't have a clue about what we are going to do when we land in China but it is sure gonna be fun getting there." "Yeah," said Matt. "I think we maybe in over our heads on this one."

The swirling winds blew the long blond hair into the face of the slim middle aged man who approached Will and Matt as they reached the jet. The man extended his hand to Matt. "Aloha, welcome to Hawaii. The name's Jack, I'm the pilot of this bird he said, as he pointed his thumb over his shoulder. You must be Matt." "Yes, I am. And this is my partner Will." "Nice to meet you Will." Will and Jack also shook hands. Matt checked his watch. "Jack we are in a bit of a hurry." "Say no more my friend. I have already been briefed. Come this way and I will stow your gear, give you guys the fifty cent tour of the craft and we will be on our way. Do either of you guys have some papers for me?" "Oh yea." Matt stopped to take the documents out of his back pocket to hand them to Jack. Will was still admiring the G4 while Jack checked the paper work. "Hey Jack, how fast can she go?" "Well, Will not as fast as that bird over there that you came in. The cruising speed for this baby is about 550 miles per hour but what she lacks in speed is made up in style. Wait until you see the inside." Before you could say Aloha the plane was airborne. "Wow," said Matt. "Jack wasn't kidding. Look at this Will. Leather seats, movies, CD's, computers and look at the food. I am way ahead of you Matt." Matt and Will stuffed themselves on jumbo shrimp, lobster, crabs and red stripe beer. Will thumbed through the music collection. "Not much here," he said while still searching. "No Marvin, no Stevie, no Diana Ross, no Martha and the Vandellas, not even a Jackson Five, ah forget it. Matt you pick something." Thinking back to his earlier conversation with Will, Matt put on Fleetwood Mac's "Over My Head". When Will caught on to the lyrics he turned from the window to Matt. "Not funny partner. We will be landing soon and Eric will be expecting us to bring back more than a few blades of grass." There was the sound of a ping over the PA system. "It was Jack. Listen guys, I just got off the horn with D.C. You guys must be pretty important. The Chinese Government has provided us with a helicopter. I have been instructed to chopper you guys over to the Olympic Ball Park where you will be given IDs and escorted into the park by Olympic Security Personnel. The CIA will take you to the hotel when you're done. They are en route but I guess you guys were too hard to keep up with."

At 6:45 p.m. The helicopter landed in the parking lot next to the mysterious field. Matt and Will had taken a few aerial shots but everything looked just as it did on the White House photos. Will noticed an elderly man wearing a traditional Asian blue silk outfit sitting on a bench smoking a corncob pipe. His glasses were wire rimmed and he stared intently as Matt and Will entered the stadium. "Hey, Will besides the grass do you notice anything different?" Will looked around. "The only thing I see is a bunch of baffled and confused people carrying equipment that I don't recognize and speaking languages I don't understand." Will paused for a beat. "Okay, I give up. What is it?" "It's the temperature Will. This is an outdoor stadium but it's at least 10% warmer in here than it is outside." Will thought for a moment then offered an explanation. Well, first of al, l we have less wind you know the seats are blocking the breeze, and second of all, this equipment these guys are lugging around is bound to give off some heat. Come on Matt. Let's get these shots before we loose the light. You take this side and I will work over here. We will meet back here in thirty minutes. Oh, don't forget to grab some grass and a soil samples."

Will and Matt collected and photographed all that they could and headed to the parking lot to find their ride to the hotel. When they reached the lot the stranger in the silk pajama looking outfit walked over to them. Just as he was about to speak, a black SUV with darkened windows pulled up between them. It was their ride. The CIA agents got out to identify themselves and help load the equipment. When they were done Matt walked to the other side of the car to talk to the stranger but he was nowhere to be found. *That's strange* he thought. The men drove to the Grand Hyatt checked in, dropped off their belongings and went to dinner with the CIA in tow. "Dag, Matt are these suits going to follow us all over town?" "Afraid so," he answered. "President Walker thinks I might get snatched." "Fine," said Will, "but I am not buying them dinner." On the way back to the hotel Matt purchased a thermometer. "What's that for?" Will asked. "It's for telling how hot or how cold it is." He looked at Will and laughed. "Matt, why can't you let it go? Besides, we are going home tomorrow after we see the Great Wall." "Come on Will, humor an old pal. I just wanna take one more look at that ball field before we go okay." Will knew that Matt would not give up until he agreed to go back. "Okay fine. But the Great Wall would have to wait."

At the crack of dawn, Matt was awakened by a pounding on the door. It was the American Ambassador to China along with the agents from the CIA. After a brief introduction he told Matt to get dressed. "Sorry to wake you at this hour. I've already rousted your co-worker Will. We could not chance using the phone lines, wiretaps you know. There been a development at the stadium. It appears

that the field of grass has been transformed over night and into just abo
color imaginable. You and your partner need to get over there before the word
gets out and the place gets trampled by the scientists and God knows who else.
The agents will drive you to the heliport and Jack will fly you over to save time."
The five men walked out of the hotel where several cabs were parked. "Agent
Harris will bring the car around. I am going to grab a cab. I didn't want to wake
my driver at this hour." Matt paid little attention to the ambassador; he was
focused on the man just on the opposite side of the water fountain in front of the
hotel. "There he is again," said Matt. The ambassador turned to Will. "What is
he talking about?" Will pointed across the driveway towards the fountain. "The
guy in the pajamas over there." The Ambassador corrected Will. "Those aren't
pajamas. That's called a Hatori." Matt started to approach the stranger when the
CIA agent stepped in front of Matt and held up the palm of his hand on Matt's
chest. "Sorry sir," he said in a deep voice. "I can't allow you to go over there. I am
responsible for your safety and we have no idea of who this individual is or what
his motives may be." Matt stepped back still staring at the man across the fountain. He said to the agent. "This is the same man that approached me at the baseball stadium yesterday. He must have a good reason for following us back to the
hotel and hanging around all night." The two men were at an impass. The
ambassador stepped up to offer a solution. "I will go over and talk to him. He
probably doesn't speak English anyway. Please, wait here." When the mysterious
stranger saw the ambassador headed his way he quickly hailed one of the waiting
cabs and speed off before the ambassador could approach him.

The helicopter ride was a short hop from Beijing. It was barely daylight when
they arrived. The view inside the stadium was spectacular. Everywhere you
looked there were orchids all different colors red, yellow, pink, orange, white, and
blue. The colorful tapestry stretched from one end to the other. Everything was
just as the ambassador described except for one major detail. From the air it was
impossible to miss. The ballpark had become one large crop circle. Eric's instincts
were right on the money. Aliens, now Matt and Will were in their element. They
knew exactly what to do. After all the photos were taken and new samples were
collected, Matt checked the temperature inside the park. "Eighty degrees all the
way around." he said to Will. They walked outside the stadium and Matt took
another reading sixty six degrees just as I thought. "The aliens must have found a
way to control the climate to protect the flowers." Matt said looking up from the
thermometer to Will. "Yeah, but the question is what aliens, ours or the other
guys. I'm calling Eric." Will took out his cell phone. "What time is it on the East
Coast, Matt?" "Does it matter?" Matt responded. "Wake his ass up. This could

be the other shoe about to drop, a big shoe. Tell him we need to get home quick. We can't afford to send this over the web. And tell him to get a hold of Art. I know that his grandmother is not feeling well, but right now we need him more. Have you noticed that this crop circle is very different from any of the others that we have ever seen?" Before Will could answer Matt the CIA men came over to help load the equipment. Jack maneuvered the chopper out of the parking lot. "Look at them down there. Like bees to honey. When you guys first came into here there were barely twenty people here. Now there must be at least a hundred." Matt was holding for Eric, he passed the thermometer to Will as they flew over the baseball stadium. "Will, eighty five degrees."

CHAPTER 12

▼

SOMETHING WICKED
THIS WAY COMES

The five jumbo screens were switched on as everyone maneuvered around the large table to find the seat with the placard that bared their name. CIA, FBI, FEMA, Homeland Security, you name it they were all there. Will, Matt, Art and Sara had already taken their seats before the President and Vice President joined the group. The President made a few remarks then turned things over to Art. He cleared his throat then directed everyone's attention to the center screen. "Three days ago, Matt and Will took these photographs at the Ball Park in China. This crop circle is unlike any that we have ever seen or deciphered. I have divided it into quarters with the first two on the left screens and the second two to the right. The symbols on screen one indicate location, longitude and latitude. Screen two shows the time. We have learned from other crop circles that 2400 indicates midnight. The third screen shows the date, and the final screen contained a very brief message. This is the most simplistic crop circle that anyone on our team has ever come across."

President Walker was not a patient man. As a child he would always skip to the ending of the book before reading a whole story. "So Art, what exactly are you trying to tell us. Well, sir. Art took a deep breath before continuing. What I am saying is that you have until September 22nd to polish the silverware and breakout the good China because we are about to have visitors." A buzz of conversation broke out around the table. The President looked at Art then at the screens. "How sure are you about this son?" "We are very sure, Mr. President. This message was designed so that we could not misinterpret its meaning. It was like placing a neon sign in the desert at midnight with no moonlight. The flowers, the location, the timing of the event to the Olympics, it all indicates that they wanted to be sure that we got this one right." "Mr. President, if I may interrupt." Eric stood over the controls next to Bob. "These may be aliens but, they are not <u>our</u> aliens. We definitely have a new player." Bob run the slides. "At my request, Matt, Art and Will loaded every crop circle photographed in the last ten years into our database. Of the thousands of circles checked, not one matches this one for the type of flowers, patterns, use of a man made venue, climate control, grass, etc." While the Vice President spoke images of all the crop circles Eric spoke of flashed across the screens behind him. "I see," said the President. He turned back to Art. "When can we expect to meet these fellows?" "According to the coordinates they will arrive in front of the United Nations building at midnight on the day of the Autumnal Equinox, September 22nd of this year sir." Will leaned over toward Matt. "That sound you hear is the other shoe dropping. Look at Walker's face. He's not buying it." The President looked around the table. First at Eric, then Matt, Will, then back to Eric. "Are you people absolutely sure that these are not the same aliens? And if so what can we do about it?" Matt thought it was time to refresh the President's memory. "Mister President as you recall the terms layed out by the alien council strictly forbids us from receiving any outside help. If we expose these visitors we can kiss all of our butts goodbye. My guess is that these are the Otarians, the same bunch involved with the bottom dwellers who tried to sabotage our ships. They know that we have never had any contact with the Lazonias or the Otarians for that matter. So if we expose ourselves…" Matt stopped in mid sentence. "Our best bet is to play out their little charade and stay the course. I suggest we play dumb. For all we know this could be a test of some kind. The Lazonias would never reveal themselves to us after trying so hard to keep their identity secret." He finished. "A brief message, just four words: It said "we come with news." It did not say good news or bad just news." "Well, good work people." The President thanked everyone for coming and asked Mrs. Robinson to contact the Ambassador of China. "Yes sir," replied Mrs. Robinson. "Should I also contact your advisors to set up the press conference sir?" "No Mrs. Robinson, I will be leaving that up to the Chinese." Will and Matt overheard the President's conversation with Mrs. Robinson. Will approached Walker. "Please tell me that you are not going to give the Chinese all the credit for our hard work." "Okay Will," I won't tell you. "However, I will tell you this. In exchange for their corporation in letting you and Matt enter their air space and wander around their country for three days, I had to promise them they would be the first to know whatever we found out. You can be sure that within a heart beat from the time I give them the information about the alien visit that they will take the credit. That's just the way it is." President Walker gathered up his papers and locked them in his briefcase. He then turned back to Art and Matt. "We are treading on thin ice fellows. When it breaks, as I am sure it will, the Chinese can also take the blame. Have a good day gentlemen." He smiled, turned and headed for the elevator. Will shook his head. "That is one shrewd S.OB."

Art stopped by Will's place on the way home to have a beer and discuss today's meeting. He was worried. "Thanks for the beer mate, nice and cold. This is just what I need right about now. I don't know Will, what if we are wrong? What if this is a message from the Planetary Alliance and we have been found out? "Sorry folks but the deals off. Have a nice but short life." "Art calm down." Will eased back in his recliner. "When did you say your wife was coming home?" "In two days," said Art. "Why?" "So she can take your mind off things for a while. You worry way too much. Are all British guys like you?" "Come on Will, give me a break. This is not did I forget to turn off the bathtub worry. This is end of the world worry. There's a huge difference. I don't see how you can be so calm." "Listen, Art. When I was growing up my mom used to always tell me that there are three things that you can never have enough of faith, patience, and hope. I know that God has sorted things out for us, all we need to do is follow the path." Art took a sip from the bottle and pulled the curtain back to get a better view from the window. "Bloody Hell, Will, I think you had better get over here; I think I may have just found your Chinaman. Or rather he just found us." Will dashed over to the window nearly knocking Art's beer onto the floor. "Son of a gun."

Will called Matt on the phone. "Matt, you will never guess who's outside my window." Matt did not take Will seriously but decided to play along. "Okay," said Matt. "Ah, Halle Berry, J. Lo, and Janet Jackson." "Come on man. Cut the crap. It's the mystery guy. You know the one from China." Matt tone turned serious. "Will, whatever you do, do not let him out of your sight I will be right there." The Chinaman was reluctant to come inside with Will but he felt that it might be better than standing in an open area where he could be spotted and reported as a prowler by the neighbors. "I wish to speak to Mr. Matthew. I have a very important message for his ears only." Will offered him a seat and a Pepsi. "You must be hot from standing out in the sun. Mr. Matthew is on his way. He has a lot of questions to ask you Mr...?" "Who I am is not important." said the stranger. "I could not risk talking to him in the presence of others. I have been told that the African and Englishmen are trustworthy but the others." He shook his head.

Minutes later, there was a pounding on the door. "That must be Matt." "Ah, Mr. Matthew it is a pleasure to meet you at last." The man bowed slightly and Matt found himself bowing in return. The Asian man adjusted his royal blue silk garment and sat down. "I am an astrologer by trade. It is my chosen profession but telepathy; that is a gift. Three and a half weeks ago, I was at my modest observatory on the hill in the countryside when I began to hear the voice of a female. It was late at night and not a soul in sight for miles. It did not take very long for me to realize that the communication was telepathic in nature. Over the next three nights, I learned the identity of the person to whom I was hearing. She said that you would know her as well. Her name is Nyssa." Matt looked at Will and Art. He nodded to acknowledge that he had known the name. "She said that she sought me out because she could not risk communication with you directly. Somehow, she knew that you would be at the stadium. She implores you to use your key, if you do my words will right true. She said if not, you and the world would be in grave danger. She then instructed me to draw the palm prints of two hands. The first shows the symbol of infinity. She called this the hand of trust. The second depicts a triangle. This is the hand of deceit and to be avoided at all costs. I did not understand her reference of the key. She said that you would understand its significance. I often meditate when the moon is full as it was during this time because the sky is bright and it is sometimes difficult to gaze at the stars above. As I have mentioned, I chart the stars and what I have discovered troubles me greatly. On the day of the Autumnal Equinox, an event will take place that will put to motion a series of events. The end result will be catastrophic loss of life unequaled in the history of humanity. It is written in the stars, you only need to know where to look." Matt excused himself and called Will and Art into the kitchen.

Will gave Matt a nudge. "Yo, do you think it's a good idea to leave him alone out there? You know he's like vapor. He could just disappear on us again." "We won't be gone that long." said Matt. "Did you guys hear what he just said? He knows everything. This fellow is the real deal. About ten percent of Lazonias have been genetically engineered altered at conception to be telepathic." Will and Art gave Matt a look. "Don't ask me how I know, I just do okay. Things must be getting hot back at the homestead so instead of risking another visit T'zar probably sent Nyssa and Lyssa to find someone to warn us. They knew we would be sent to China to investigate the crop circle so they found a way to get a message to us without exposing themselves." "You're right," Art said. "But he doesn't have a clue who Nyssa is, and that bit about people dying, we already know that the bottom dwellers may be toast." Will jumped into the conversation. "You all are forgetting a few things. He said that that Autumnal Equinox would be the turning point to disaster, so he could not be talking about the bottom dwellers. He knew before we interpreted the crop circle that something was up. We gotta find out who this cat is before he vanishes again. He could be a plant." "Too late." Art was peeping around the corner to check on the mystery man. "I mean he's gone again." The Chinaman was nowhere to be found, but he did not leave them empty handed. On the coffee table were three sheets of paper. Two with hand print drawings and on the bottom sheet was an astrological chart. The first hand was the infinity symbol; the second was a triangle with a straight line under the can of cola. Will gathered the papers and used a pen to put the empty can into a baggie. Matt put his hands on his hips. "Well boys," he said starring at the couch where the messenger sat. "Every time we think we have things figured out another mystery develops and this one is a doozie. Time to call Eric."

The stress of being the go between Walker and Matt was beginning to take it's toll on Eric. Matt sat on the edge of Eric's desk and gave him the details of the encounter with the Asian visitor. "Look Matt, you know that I will do whatever I can to help the team but there are limits. Palm reading, astrology, and telepathy. Do you really expect me to waltz into Walker's office eleven days before the first official alien visit and tell him that they are not to be trusted because of some phantom Chinese guy's story? I need something more concrete. It's a good thing the Chinese government is in a good mood these days. They are running the prints from the soda can. If we can bag your mystery man then maybe we can go to the President. You said yourself, that this could be a test, a setup. The Planetary Alliance or whoever the hell these guys are may have your people in custody and could be using this to welch on the deal. We could be up the creek without a planet if we don't play this one right. Don't forget the Otarians, they screwed us once already using the bottom dwellers to cripple our ships. Look Matt, I got another meeting in ten minutes. Every ruler, Emperor, President, and Prime Minister will probably be stopping by. When I hear something on the prints I will let you know. In the meantime, keep digging okay buddy?" "Thanks, Eric." They shook hands and Matt took off.

News of the alien visit to Earth spread like wildfire. As the President predicted the Government of China wasted no time in taking credit for everything. News media from all around the world descended on New York City and Washington D.C while the White House staff kicked it into overdrive. Art, Will and Matt were at a stand still. The prints from the Pepsi can did not match any of the prints in China's computer systems. Eric chose not tell the President about the Chinaman. It was the Sunday before the big Alien-Human meet and greet in the Big Apple and Matt was dozing off in his favorite chair. The sound of church bells roused him from his sleep. He rubbed his face and leaned forward in the chair staring into space. He could hear the words of the stranger. "Use your key and my words will ring true." Matt asked Art and Will to come over. When they arrived he told them of his vision. "I was aboard the Silver Unicorn. Sitting at the dinning table only this time there was no food. Across from me sat Onan, Lsyta, and Nyssa. One by one they laid their hands on the table face up. At frist, I thought it was a dream but then I realized that it was a conformation of the message delivered by the Chinaman. In the center of each palm was the symbol of Infinity. They symbol of the Lazons. It symbolizes "The Hand of Trust"." Matt opened his hand to illustrate the point. "Okay then," said Art. "That's it. The proof we have been waiting for but why wasn't T'zar at the table?" Will looked at Matt's and Art. He spoke in a low but calm voice. "He was," said Will. "That's how Matt was able to see the others. Nyssa must have told T'zar that he and Matt are connected. He used his eyes to show Matt the visions of the hands." "Wow!" Art sat straight up. "That makes sense. This is entering a whole new level of weirdness. Now if I can only find that slippery Chinaman we can warn the President." Matt picked up the drawing of the hand with the triangle. "This can only mean one thing." "Yeah," said Will. "Don't say it." Matt put down the paper and watched the reporter on the television standing in front of the barricades at the United Nations building. "The Otarians are coming. The second trap is about to be sprung and there's not much we can do about it."

After kicking around a few ideas and trying to guess what the Otarians were up to. Matt walked Art and Will to the White House parking lot. The halls were filled with dignitaries from every corner of the globe. Most were wearing traditional native garb India, Africa, Mexico, Australia, Spain, Switzerland, and dozens more. The three men ran into Eric along the way. They pulled him aside to give him an update. In mid-sentence, Matt stopped as he spotted something familiar across the room. "That's it." Eric seemed puzzled. "What?" Matt became more excited. He pointed across the crowded room. "The guy from China! That's what he was wearing! But the color was different." Eric attempted to correct him. "Nice try friend, but that is the Japanese Ambassador not China. Come with me. I will introduce you." After the introductions, Art inquired about the Ambassador's attire. "Pardon my ignorance. Mr. Ambassador I was admiring your outfit. What is it called?" "Ah, thank you for the complement. This is a

Hatori." Matt and Will had made a major blunder. They rushed back to Matt's quarters while Eric put in the call. Will rarely beat up on himself, but this was one of the times. "How could I be so short sighted? He yelled. Hatori! The Chinese Ambassador gave us that name so I assumed that the garment and the guy were from China. All this time wasted." Matt lay stretched out on the sofa staring at the ceiling. He was too frustrated to speak. Art tried to console them. "Guys, guys, even Willie Mays struck out sometimes." Eric joined the group after making the call. "This one's going to be close. The Japanese are running the prints we should have our guy or at least his identity by tomorrow. The President leaves for New York at ten a.m. He wants me to accompany him on this one. I have a plane on stand by for you three in case you get something and need to get to the UN in a hurry. Look at the bright side. There's still time. We could have gotten this information a week late instead of a day early. I'll be in touch."

By morning, Eric decided to send for the team and setup a makeshift H.Q in New York. His decision was prompted by the revelation behind the match to the prints on the can of cola. He kept Will, Art and Matt in the dark until they arrived. After taking them to a private room not far from the UN he gave them the news. "We can speak freely here. This will be our base of operations until further notice. Here is why I sent for you." He handed everyone duplicate documents with the picture of the man they had been looking for. "The Japanese came through for us, he said this is Mr. Kandagawa. Until January 1995, he was the top astrologer to all the movers and shakers in Japan. Then he simply dropped out of sight." "Until now." added Will. Matt knew there was more to the story. He held the paper out toward Eric. "Okay, what happened in ninety-five?" Eric smiled. "Thought you'd never ask. An Earthquake happened, one of the worst in Japanese history happened on January 17th to be exact. You see two weeks before the quake Kandagawa went to the Japanese officials to warn them but no one would listen. He even went to the local papers and TV stations. After the quake, he went underground. I'm guessing that he feared the government would not want him speaking to the press or maybe the whole experience was just too much for him to take, anyway here we are all these years later and he's back with an even more ominous warning. This guy is no joke, we know what happened the last time he was ignored and I don't intend to make the same mistake." "Do we know where he is?" "No, Art. He is very good at not being found when he wants to disappear, but I do feel that we now have enough to go to the President. The aliens will be here soon. We don't have much time."

In a few short hours, the aliens would be arriving. Hundreds of thousands of people from all over the world have traveled to New York hoping to get a glimpse of the visitors. The atmosphere was festive almost party-like. Thousands of people, many who had camped outside the police barricades played music and shared stories of alien encounters. The CIA, FBI and members of Homeland Security mingled through the crowds while other officers took up positions with high powered weapons a top the skyscrapers facing the UN. There was a chill in the air. The forecast called for light rain however this did not dampen the excitement of the throngs of spectators. All day long, a steady stream of limousines carrying world leaders made their way through the final checkpoint before proceeding to the front entrance. Among the first to arrive were Egypt, France, Lybia, Italy, Norway, Spain, and Jamaica. Each with their country's flags fluttered proudly on the front hood. Military helicopters kept a close watch overhead while all other aircraft were warned of the no-fly zone. It took a while for Matt, Art, and Will to settle in. It was evening before they heard from Eric again. "Hey Eric, what's up?" When Art and Matt heard who Will was speaking to they put in on the speakerphone. "Hi Will, the President has been in meetings, press conferences, and photo ops all day. I finally got a chance to speak with him in private. He understands the gravity of the situation but is not sure how to proceed tonight. He also said and I quote "They are sending me into the ring with both hands tied behind my back." We are going to have to wait until tonight to find out how to proceed." Eric explained. "We don't know what they want. Unless you guys can offer some guidance we are on hold." Matt leaned in on the speaker. "Eric, the only thing that I can suggest is to try to get a good look of their hands." "Roger that, Matt. I will give you guys a buzz around eleven. See ya."

Later that night, Art braved the mass of people to bring back dinner for the team. He struggled to get inside with all the bags of hot food. "Whew! It's getting quite nippy out. A little bugger on the lift tried to nick the bag with the fries. Well anyway supper's here. Can one of you give me a hand?" Matt and Will were watching the live coverage at the UN down the street. "What did I miss?" He asked Will as he passed him one of the bags. "Nothing much, the Crown Prince is wrapping up his speech. Pretty boring stuff but it's not as if we have a choice. All the games have been canceled. Every station in the world is broadcasting this." Art strained his neck to get a better view of the television. "Oh, look. It's the Queen Mum. Turn it up." The reporter was giving a wrap up. "Let's send it upstairs to Kim." "Thank you, Lisa. We are on the roof topwith a couple of UFO experts. As you can see from all the telescopes and cameras pointing skyward we should get the first pictures of the visitor's space ship as this historic event as conditions began to unfold. I am being told that the leaders are beginning to take their places on the front steps. The workers here have apparently set up a tarp to protect the speakers from the elements while they are at the podium. A red carpet has also been rolled out from the steps all the way to First Ave. I am not sure if rolling out the carpet so early was a good idea. It has started to drizzle here in Manhattan and the dignitaries have broken out the umbrellas."

Eric called around eleven but brought no new news. Tonight was Art's night to shine. He was in his element. "Okay boys," he said rubbing his hands together. "Let' go over this once more." He pointed to the bank of computer screens to the left. "Matt, this is your station. These are real time images from telescopes as far away as India. Give us a shout if anything turns up. Will, you are over here." He placed his hands on the blue phone. "This is a direct line to S.E.T.I. Next to it is the most powerful short wave radio that I could get my hands on at such short notice. You both need to monitor the television screens behind me as well. We have cameras and microphones in various key locations around the area. I will monitor everything that goes on once they arrive. We may only get one shot at gathering information on these guys so stay alert. In less tan an hour, we will know if they are friend or foe. If they are the latter, we are going to need every edge that we can get." Will slapped Art on the back. "I heard that," he said. The next forty minutes were uneventful, but at 11:55 Will heard the naval helicopter pilot over the radio say "We have movement in the water. I repeat, there is movement in the East River. Do you copy base?" "This is base, we copy. Please elaborate." "Yes, base. I see green, white and amber lights. Getting brighter now." Heavy waves were crashing the shoreline.

Matt pointed to one of the television screens. Apparently, MSNBC had the foresight to place a camera toward the river. "Look guys!" Matt shouted "there they are. The massive space vessel slowly emerged from the cold icey waters of the East River. Her steel black hull glistened in the night sky as it banked right and began moving faster as it gained altitude. It rose above the UN then continued to climb higher than the empire state building. The crowd went wild. People clapped cheered and danced in the street. There were thousands of flashing cameras blinking on and off like fire works in the night. The ship glided quietly through rain until it was positioned directly over the United Nations. The vessel was so large that it protected everyone in the streets from the rain. Without warning two oval panels on the underside of the ship side opened. Two smaller ships emerged and began their decent onto the blocked off area of the street below. Will glanced at the clock. "Midnight. At least they are prompt." Matt joined Will at the window. He nodded in agreement. "Yeah, and they do know how to make an entrance." Will and Matt watched all the action from the window while Art operated the robotic cameras. The mini ships touched down roughly two hundred feet apart. They appeared to be the same color and material as the mother ship above. A coat of arms adorned each ship on the right side of the doors.

Exiting the first ship, were twenty tall slender blonde haired women wearing long flowing powder blue gowns trimmed in gold. The flowers in their hair were also blue and gold. Each gracefully carried a shinny cobalt blue ball slightly lager than the size of a basketball. The power source inside gave off a soft glow. The women lined the carpet on both sides with the lights then formed one large circle in between the two ships. In contrast to the first ship were the men. Thirty strong rugged military men marched quickly onto the street. All of the men had dark hair and a few had short beards. Each took their place beside one of the glowing balls. They wore black pants with a thin blood red stripe down the side and red shirts. They each carried a flag and showed the coat of Arms Identical to the one on the ships. The three quarter length black capes were also trimmed in red. If it were not for the wind blowing the capes, you would not have noticed the weapons concealed under them. The remaining guards took up positions on the outer circle facing the crowds while the women looked inward ignoring the presence of the men; neither, the men or women spoke a single word. The crowds enjoyed every second of the arrival proceedings. Every pair of eyes on the east side of Manhattan was glued on the ship. An extremely large ball of blue crackling static began to form directly underneath the space ship. As the static electricity inside the ball began to build, the ball grew larger and larger. Suddenly, there was the deafening sound of rolling thunder as the big blue magnetic ball fell rapidly to Earth. Some in the crowd covered their ears while others gasped and quickly backed away. The women from the visiting ship simply fell to one knee as if they were given a secret command for their ears only. The ball hit the ground directly in the center of the circle with a loud thunderclap that could be heard for miles. When the ball collapsed a strange mist hugged the ground like the kind you see burning off a country field on a cool spring morning. The smell of lavender filled the air. It seemed to have a calming effect on the crowd. Appearing from the mist in the center of the circle stood the Supreme Chancellor, ruler of the planet.

Flanked just slightly behind him were two well-built athletic types carring locked cases the size of microwave ovens. One case was bronze the other silver. The leader proceeded down the red carpet waving to the crowd as he passed. He was a tall man with a short white beard and salt and pepper hair that flowed down the back of his neck. He wore Royal Blue pants with a matching coat that stopped at the knee. The guards stood like statues as the flags a top the six-foot poles fluttered in the night. It truly was a spectacular sight to see. After being greeted by the head of the UN, the visitor took the podium. "Greetings people of

Earth." Once again, the crowd went into frenzy. "I am Rotart I, Supreme leader of the planet Lazon. I have traveled a great many galaxies to be with you tonight. I carry a message that will bring joy and jubilation to all humans. For many decades, our finest scientists have been seeking a solution that will deliver you from the destruction of your planet. I am most happy to announce that a solution has been discovered and implemented. Planet Earth has been saved."

Matt, Art, and Will watched in utter disbelief as the crowd went wild. People wept, jumped, and shouted. Rotart had to wait for quite a while before he was able to be heard again. When it was over Art turned to the others and said. "Will I guess we don't need the pictures now. It's clear that his guy is a phony as a three dollar bill." "Yeah," Will agreed. "He's got a lot of balls. We were warned that something big was going to happen but I would have never thought that they would try something this brazen. Do you think our leaders are buying it Matt?" Matt turned to the television screens. "I don't know Will, but it doesn't matter because everyone else sure is. Just look at them." Matt pointed to the seven televisions on the wall. On each screen the scene was the same. Hugh crowds were celebrating around the world. Will dialed the phone. "We are in big trouble," he said while making the call. Eric has to get a hold of Walker. There was a knock on the door. It was the agent with the first batch of pictures. Art thumbed through them quickly and pulled two from the stack. "Well, mates. I am sure that this won't be a shock to either of you. This Rotart fellow is about as dodgy as they come" He passed one photo to Matt and the other to Will. It showed the palm of the Supreme leader as he waived to the people. There could no longer be any doubt. The symbol of the triangle was as clear as a bell. This was the hand that the chinaman warned them about.

CHAPTER 13

▼

LIKE LAMBS TO THE SLAUGHTER

For the fist time, President Walker was fully on board with Eric and the team. He compared the alien leader's manner to that of a used car salesman. The meeting with the President didn't get underway until well after four a.m. Walker looked grim. "Guys, I have to tell you all that you were spot on from the very beginning. This guy is so slimy it's a wonder that he can sit down without sliding to the floor." Eric consulted some notes he scribbled down on a pad. "At an earlier meeting, Rotart I said he would only be here for three days. The dinner is tomorrow at eight. That's when he is going to open the two boxes. Well, Mr. President. What's our next move? At least half of the world leaders are buying this guy's bull." "Well Eric, we continue to play along. I can talk to our British friends as well the Israelis, and the Mexicans. They can be trusted. I will try to corner this joker at dinner and confront him about the hand. We still have the mystery boxes to deal with. We will just have to see what other tricks the Otarian has up his sleeve. Eric please get a hold of the press secretary and Mrs. Robinson. For now, we stay the course. Put the word out that I want those ships completed on time. I will not risk American lives on the word of a stranger. Everyone get some sleep. It's been a long day and tomorrow is going to be even longer."

A copy of the New York Post was delivered to Will's hotel room along with his breakfast. The headlines read <u>Alien Savior Arrival Wows Spectators</u>. Will could not believe how gullible people had become. Before he could finish his eggs and sausages, Art dropped in to talk to him before the meeting. "Morning, mate." Will handed Art the paper. "What's so good about it? Have you read that? Rotart show s up. He puts on a light show and everybody's IQ drops to 50." "It's not that simple, Will. People believe Rotart because they don't want to leave Earth. He's just telling them what they want to hear. When I was a child, I believed in Father Christmas because I wanted the toys. Keep in mind that the public does not know what we do". Will looked at Art as he reached over into Will's plate and speared his last sausage with a fork. He waved it in front of Will while he spoke. It's up to President "Walker and the others to set things straight. Just give it some time, Will." "That's the problem Art. Time is the one thing we don't have."

The team spent most of the day pouring over the photographs and discussing last night's activities. Art passed a few more pictures over to Matt. "Not much to look at, mate. Clever little devils, sneaking up the river like that so that they would not be tracked. I am more certain than ever that they came directly from Neptune's Eye. Long journey my foot." Matt waved one of the pictures in Art's direction. "You're looking at this all wrong. It's not what you see it's what you don't. The less they show us the more suspicious people will become. Look at this." Matt began reading from the morning paper. "Alien leader Rotart I forbids contact with his entourage. I think we all know why. I heard President Walker has made sure that he will be seated next to Rotart at dinner."

Walker wasted no time working on Rotart as they dined. "I was wondering," said the President "Why is there an I after your name? Is it a middle initial?" "No," replied Rotart. "It's more like a designation. I am the Ninth ruler from my bloodline using your alphabet that would be I; on my home planet we commonly use the numeral in place of the letter." "I see," said Walker. "Like Harry the Eighth. I also noticed your hand. I don't want to be rude but what is that symbol?" By this time all conversation around the table had stopped. Everyone was curious but didn't want to ask. Rotart I held up his hand as if he were preforming a show and tell in grade school. "Thousands of years ago, our people developed what you refer to as genetic engineering. We were able to eliminate most diseases. As a side benefit, the planets in our galaxy decided that each race would be identified by marking the hand prior to birth to identify ones planet of origin. Each race came up with a symbol that they feel proudly reflects the meaning of their existence. This line under the triangle represents the land. The left bar of the triangle is for the sun, this one the rain and the last is air for without these things there could be no life." After dessert the leaders filed into a large room.

Rotart I was introduced and he summoned his bodyguards to bring the mysterious boxes to the stage. "For years, we have watched the humans struggle and
finally you have put your differences aside by working together for the common
goal of preservation. My people and I are touched by your progress in this universe that we all share. For your efforts, and to help you to continue on this path
we are giving you a gift. He walked over to the table and placed his hand on the
bronze box. This is a water purifier it is much like the ones on the ships that you
have built. There is one significant difference: This machine can purify fifty liters
of sea water per minute." Rotart I could tell that the group was impressed. He
waited for the buzz of conversation that broke out in the room to subside.. Next,
he moved over to the silver box. "As I have previously mentioned we have kept a
close eye on Earth. As you are aware in the year 2003, you experienced many
power failures. This generator will provide you with an endless source of power
for at least a hundred of your years." Again, the conversation through the room
picked up. Cuba's dictator yelled from the back row. "What's the catch?" "There
is no catch," Rotart replied. "As you humans are found of saying it's free of
charge. However, since we cannot manufacture thousands of these overnight we
have decided that we would be more generous to those countries that are generous to others. Let me explain…" Walker looked at Eric. *Here it comes,* he thought
to himself. Rotart I walked back to the center of the stage. "You no longer have
need of your ships yet you have millions of humans without proper shelter or
food. We can reprogram the ships to fly short distances and secure them permanently to the ground. Once the conversion is complete the ships would never be
able to fly again but your people, millions of people will no longer suffer the
harsh winters or brutal summer out in the elements. Your homeless problem
would be solved overnight. So those who give first get first. In two days time, I
will return to home with a list of countries that are willing to convert their ships
immediately. We will begin manufacturing the machines at once. In exactly one
year, I will return with a fleet of ships to personally make the delivery." Rotart
could see that not everyone was convinced. Upon my arrival last night I noticed a
small vessel in the harbor. "I was told it was called the Queen Mary I. I feel that a
demonstration is in order. Tomorrow, I will provide those who remain skeptical
with a demonstration. We have received permission to power the vessel using one
of our generators. We will also setup a water tank to demonstrate the purifier as
well."

Very few governments were eager to take Rotart I up on his offer but France
and Spain jumped at the chance to acquire the new technology. Bright and early
next morning everyone gathered on the banks of the East River to watch Rotart

work his magic. He started the demonstration with an enthusiastic welcome. "Greetings citizens of Earth." With two of his bodyguards standing slightly behind him, he directed the attention of the group to a very large transparent tank. "As you can see, our host has been gracious enough to provide us with this container to demonstrate this useful piece of equipment. With the touch of this button, I will purify 5,000 liters of river water." Rotart pressed the button to start the machine. "As you can see, the water is clean and ready to drink. Please proceed to witness the completion of this demonstration."

After successfully completing the demonstration, Rotart managed to gain a few more converts. Germany, Cuba, South Korea, and Poland had signed on. Dozens of countries were on the fence including Canada, Spain, Greece and Mexico. The President flew back to Washington to confer with his advisors and brief congress. During the flight home he huddled with the Vice President. "Eric, I have to admit this is a very tempting offer. Have you considered all the good we could do, the millions of people we could help?" "Yes, Mr. President I have, but taking into consideration the inside info that we have on this snake oil salesmen. I keep thinking about the old saying, a bird in the hand is worth two in the bush. I guess what I am saying sir, is that we can't afford to trust this guy. He's trying way too hard." "Yes Eric, I hear what you are saying but take a look at this poll that was released a few hours ago. Sixty eight percent of Americans think we should take the offer, and fourteen percent are undecided." "Yes, Mr. President, I admit that Rotart puts on one hell of a show but we know he's bogus. With all due respect, sir, you must stay the course on this one. Matt, Art, and Will have done their homework. I trust them with my life."

Meanwhile in an attempt to woo more of the world's leaders Rortart offered a tour of the Mother ship to those who were leaning towards signing the deal. By the end of the day, one phrase was heard repeatedly. "We would not commit until the American's do." This was very frustrating to Rotart I but he was not alone in his frustration. Members of the House and Senate were more than a little frustrated with Walker's refusal to accept the alien's offer. In an emergency session of Congress attended by the President, members from both sides of the isle bombarded the President with questions. "Mr. President the people are dancing in the streets over this wonderful news, and many countries have beaten us to the punch to get on board with this new technology, while we sit on our hands." President Walker was beginning to weaken. The polls, Congress and the Senate were all against him. He sat in the oval office pondering the day's events when the phone rang. It was Rotart. "Hello President Walker. I understand your hesitation. I too would be reluctant to accept such an offer. I hope to allay your fears by offering you an inivitation to accompany me back to my home planet so that any doubts that plague you would be put to rest. I no that this is very short notice but I must return home soon." Walker saw this as a chance to expose Rotart I and the Otarians. At the very worse he would have time to get away and think of a way to handle his critics. "Yes," he said into the phone. "I accept your very generous offer. Would you like to come to the White House for dinner tomorrow to work out the details?" "Yes, I accept your invitation, Mr. President. You have no idea of how pleased I am to hear that you will be joining me on this journey."

By the time Rotart sat down for dinner at the White House a diplomatic storm was raging. Other countries had felt slighted, left out of the trip to visit Rotart's planet. Many of those leaders were in attendance at the dinner party. One of the leaders turned to Rotart I. "Once again, the U.S has been given preferential treatment over other nations." he complained. Roart smiled. "Come now, gentlemen." He motioned with both hands as if he were trying to tamp down some invisible object. "There is a simple solution to this problem. Each of you are welcome to join us on this trip but I must caution you that because of the size of your group you will not be permitted to have your staff accompany you and as a reminder communication with my people is strictly forbidden. We will depart in twenty four hours." Once again, Rotart managed to surprise everyone at the table. His bag of tricks was endless.

William, Matt, and Art were laying in wait for Eric. When he returned to his office Matt let him have it. "Eric are you nuts! I admit that Walker is not on my list of favorite people but how could you let him agree to go with those people or whatever they are? Have you been listening to anything that we have been telling you?" Eric fired back, "Walker is a stubborn man. The decision was made before I found out! The President thinks that he can expose him by gaining intel on the trip. Look guys, I am with you. I have been from the beginning. It's out of my hands." Will reached into the inside pocket of his jacket. "Speaking of hands." He carefully unfolded the paper he pulled from his pocket and he handed it to Eric. "This was on my windshield," Will explained, check out the signature on the bottom. The message was simple. It read:

It has become clear that your President has chosen to ignore the message and warning that I have delivered. I have revealed myself to you in hopes that my creditability will prevent your President from allying himself with the aliens. He is in grave danger. Singed, Kandagawa.

Eric flipped the letter over. There was one line. "2012, Year of the Rat."

CHAPTER 14

▼

CHARADE

Walker had been second-guessing himself from the time that he and the other leaders left Earth on Rotart's ship. Everyone was surprised at the ships lavish interior. Room after room was filled with oversized pillows, large round tables that stood only a few inches from the floor and beautiful flowers in oversize vases everywhere you looked. Tapestries and painting that hung from walls were painted various shades even though most were blue and purple with gold trim. The décor was magnificent. It looked more like a flying palace than a space ship. After Rotart gave them the grand tour, each guest was assigned a personal aide who escorted them to their rooms and would tend to their needs during the trip. Rotart personally dropped off President Walker at his quarters. His aide was already waiting inside.

"Greetings, President Walker, I am called Fantana." Walker was surprised to see that Rotart had chosen a female for his aide. Up until now the Otarian women had been mostly seen and not heard. "My purpose is to see to it that you have everything you need and to guide you through out the ship for functions and dinning." She stared at Walker as if she was trying to decide whether to say something more. Walker could not help but notice that Fantana was by far the most attractive of the aliens that he had encountered, thus far. She showed Walker how to operate several gadgets in his quarters then handed him a small silver device about the size of a cigarette lighter. "Press the blue button if you need anything." Again, she gave Walker the look before turning and leaving the room. "What a strange woman." Walker mumbled to himself.

A short time later Fantana returned with several garments for the President. "The Supreme Chancellor has taken the liberty to outfit you and the other guests in more suitable attire." She placed the neatly folded stack of clothing on a nearby table next to a fruit bowl. "Thank you, but who is;" before Walker could finish the question Fantana answered, "Our leader has many titles. The one I speak of is Rotart." Fantana made President Walker feel very uncomfortable but he could not put his finger on the reason why. There was a rectangular button on the wall about shoulder high that controlled the door. She raised her hand to operate the door but paused and turned back to look at Walker. She spoke in a low ominous tone. Her friendly, bright smile was gone. She looked stoned faced and cold as she made her parting comment. "Things aren't always as they seem," she said and then turned and left the room.

Everyday since the journey began Walker and the thirty-two other world leaders would sit for hours eating, drinking and making plans for the future. Sometimes they would meet well into the night because in space you tend to loose track of the time. One night after Walker was escorted to his room, Fantana asked him to take a seat. Under normal circumstances Walker would have told her to leave. He was not used to being told what to do but he was curious to know what was on her mind. "Why are you here?" She said in a blunt voice. Walker was puzzled by the question. "What do you mean?", he asked. Fantana seemed slightly irritated. "Many of my comrades have taken great risk to warn you and your people of the impending doom of your planet. Our people warned you, the Asian seer warned you, you were warned by messages in the circles and yet here you sit. Why?" Fantana did not wait for an answer. She continued to chastise the President. "You were warned not to trust the Otarians and you along with the others have fallen prey to their trap." Walker poured himself a drink. Now he was the one starring back at Fantana. "Who are you?" he asked "I know you are not some flunky." Fantana leaped from her seat and threw her hands up in disgust. "What does it matter? It is clear from your presence that you do not believe what we have been telling you. Why continue?" Walker felt like a kid being scolded by his mother. "Because I need proof!" He shot back. "I cannot reveal what I know without exposing the Lazarions." Fantana took a few deep breaths and regained her composure. "Okay fine," she said. "Rotart cannot take you to the planet Otar. His home world is on the brink of collapse. It is overcrowded and close to running out of natural resources. In short, it is a real mess. There is growing talk on the streets of anarchy. He is very desperate, and that, my naïve friend makes him very very dangerous. My sources tell me that we are already headed to Lazon. Roatart is very crafty he knows that the time of the Triple B is rapidly approaching." "What's that?" asked Walker. "Lazon is about to celebrate the Festival of Life. It is the equivalent to your New Years. During this time, the planet Lazon is open to outsiders. BBB means no border, barricades, or boundaries until the end of the celebration of Life. Rotart would not dare show his face. It would alert the Lazarians to his devious plan. He will probably leave this ship and send Omar as his replacement. The clothes you were given upon your arrival here were also part of his plan. They were designed to help your people blend in. Do not speak of this to anyone. I must go now. My time here had been long and I will be missed." "Fantana wait. Why are you helping the Lazarians?" Fantana smiled and said. "Things are not always as they seem."

It didn't take long for the President to realize that Fantana was telling him the truth. The next day, while he and a few others were lounging on the oversized cushions discussing space travel Rotart entered looking very serious. "Greetings," he said as he looked around the room. "Pardon me, I must consult with my aide." Omar and Rotart chatted quietly on the far side of the room until all the guests arrived. Rotart stood before the group and lifted his hand outward to them. "I have requested that everyone gather here so that I can address the group as a whole. I have just been informed of a recent development that requires my attention. An emergency meeting of the council will convene in two days time. It is mandatory that I attend. Due to location and time constraints, it has become necessary for me to alter the ship's course and destination. I am sorry to inform you that we will not be going to the planet Otar as planned. I have instead made arrangements for you to tour our Omega Planet called Lazon. I am sure you will not be disappointed once you arrive. It is our festival time and you are all in for a treat. Omar has offered to stand in for me until after the meetings. I am confident that all you your questions will be answered by the end of the visit. Now, If you will excuse me, I must prepare for the meeting." Rotart and Omar made a hasty exit before anyone could question them. The general consensus in the room was that visiting one of Rotart's planets was just as good as visiting another. Only Walker was the wiser having been for warned by Fantana. It was then that he felt that he needed an ally, a human ally.

That evening Fantana escorted Walker to his room. There was a hint of a smirk on her face. Yes, she was gloating but tired not to let It show. Walker could hardly wait for the door to close. "Okay," he conceded, "You were right. Matt was right Will was right, hell even Art was right. It seems that everybody knows whats going on, but me." Fantana sighed. "We are not going to go through that again are we?" She slapped her hands on her knees and reared back in the chair. "I told you that it is for you own protection. You do not know how cunning and ruthless these people are. You..." Walker cut her off. "I demand to know right now. I can handle myself." "You can handle yourself," Fantana repeated. "Do you know what Clear is?" "No." admitted Walker. "Just as I thought." snaped Fantana. "I did not think so. It is a truth drug. Only it works in reverse. You lock yourself in a room with the intended victim and ask him questions that he does not want to answer. If Rotart or Omar gives you even a quarter oz. of this stuff they can read your mind for up to thirty minutes. Let me show you. I want you to lie to me when I ask you a question. What color are my eyes?" "Green." Walker answered. Fantana continued "You see the first thought that registered in your mind was blue then you fabricated the answer green. If I were under the influence of clear, I would have disregarded your spoken answer and correctly chosen blue. The first thought that entered your mind. This is very dangerous stuff. Imagine what would happen if several people entered the room. All those voices could drive one insane." "Okay fine," said Walker. "I will just have to make sure that Rotart doesn't lock me in a room. I want to know everything from the beginning." Fantana had run out of patience. "No! Haven't you been listening? The answer is no! Goodnight!" Fantana started toward the door when she heard Walker say "Tell me or I will expose you as a traitor." she stopped dead in her tracks. Fantana turned and stared at Walker in disbelief. "What did you say?" Walker repeated the threat. "I will expose you and your whole group if you don't tell me everything right now." "You are a fool she snapped. I do not believe you." Walker reached for the phone. "Put that down!" She ordered. Walker was about to push the button when Fantana realized that she had no choice but to comply. She could not chance risking the entire operation and exposure of her friends and relatives. For almost a half hour she told Walker the whole story but with one minor alteration. Fantana knew that Walker had never met T'zar, Onan, Nyssa, or Lyssa so she changed the names in an attempt to shield them if Walker decided to talk. Fantana crossed her legs and sat back in the chair. She waited for Walker to respond to what she had told him but Walker just sat there. "I have told you everything there is to know. The hour is late. Am I free to go?" Walker turned to Fantana. "There is still one unanswered question." Fantana looked puzzled. "President Walker I have held nothing back. What more do you require of me?" "Why?", said Walker. "Why have you betrayed your people? Money, blackmail, love? Why?" Fantana slowly walked over to President Walker and opened her hand. She gritted her teeth as she started to pull back a thin layer of skin where the triangle the symbol of Otar once was. She clenched her teeth harder as she tugged at the synthetic layer of skin. After a few moments, Walker could clearly see the infinity symbol. It was the mark of the Lazons. Fantana was a Lazorian. She gave Walker a long icy stare. "As I have told you" she said as she continued to stare at Walker, "things are not always as they seem." Fantana felt that she had failed her mission. She left without saying goodnight and without speaking another word, Fantana simply walked out.

The next few days were awkward for President Walker. Fantana would escort him to and from his quarters but refused to talk to him. Finally, they reached Lazon. Late that night Walker had a visitor. It was Fantana, "Come in. I didn't expect to see you." She walked past Walker carrying a small pouch. I have given a full report to my contact at Earth's Guardians. "I suggested that we terminate all contact with you and your people but fortunately, for you they did not see things my way." She handed Walker the pouch. "Inside you will find a device. For the lack of a better way to put it, let's call it an electronic history book. We rarely use paper. This will tell you everything about our people and this planet, our planet, Lazon, that Rotart claims as his own. I am instructed to tell you that if this book is found in your possession we will deny having given it to you. I was not here tonight. Our leaders felt that this would put an end to your constant meddling in our efforts to try to save your people." The President took the device from the bag and gave it a brief going over. "Thank you Fantana, I didn't mean…" "Don't thank me," she interrupted. "Thank Earth's Guardians. I will be going now. Goodbye, Mr. President."

At breakfast, that morning Omar was eavesdropping on the conversation between Walker and the President of Mexico. "Late night Walker?" He said with a sheepish grin. "A little shipboard romance in the works?" Walker knew Omar and those nearby could hear so he tried to play things down. "I am sure I don't know what you are talking about." said Walker. "Of course you do. That Fantana, not bad. If I were single I would have beat you to her." Walker changed the subject. "So, today is the day we get to go to the surface and see what's going on." Walker looked over to Omar but the cushion where he sat was empty. Walker was sure that Omar had heard about Fantana leaving his quarters late at night. Moreover, in a few minutes Rotart would know also.

Lazon was a beautiful planet. It was very different from Earth. Omar arrived on the planet in a separate shuttle a few minutes after the others. "I am sorry for the delay." said Omar. "Let us began. I am sure that the first thing that you noticed was the color of the sky." The sky was a powder pink color with white puffy clouds. Omar pointed to the fields where the ships had landed. There were yellow and orange flowers everywhere. "These flowers are called oxyflox. They give off a natural chemical that helps purify our air but the oxyflox alone cannot keep us free from the exhaust produced by our older vessels that use a sulfur base fuel so our scientist developed the eco mist. The eco mist enviormentalizers ring the planet just above the clouds." Everyone looked up as Omar pointed to the pink sky the mist combined with the plants cleans all impurities from the atmosphere. "The results are pinkish skies early in the day and reddish orange sky at sunset. Your timepieces are useless on this planet. Each day consists of twenty-eight hours." Lybian's ruler pointed to the building in the distance. "Omar, why have you brought us here on the countryside and not to the city?" Omar pointed to the city and said. "My friend, that is the ancestral city of the Lost. You will not learn much from a visit there. You see, it is the city of the dead. The city is totally automated. Robots run everything year round. Burial grounds are a waste of land, a luxury we cannot afford. Would you like to see?"

The mini ships transported the groups to the heart of the city. The atmosphere was eerie to say the least. No people, no noise, no music just large gray buildings looming high into the pink sky. There was a stillness in the air. Even though Omar told the group that the temperature was maintained at eighty-seven degrees the City of the Lost somehow seemed colder. Each building rose to 170 stories. The granite skyscrapers were as long and wide as a city block. Omar lead the group into a nearby building. The floor was lined left to right, top to bottom with compartments containing the deceased. In front of each, was a number and a single white candle. President Walker asked Omar about the candles. "The candles represent life," explained Omar. "At birth, every citizen is presented with a candle which is lit by the mother's candle at the child naming ceremony. The shorter candles you see here belonged to females who have bore many children. The longer steams from the males whose candles are lit only twice. Once at birth and once after death at the Festival of Lights celebration that takes place tomorrow night during the Celebration of Life." England's Prime Minister seemed intrigued by it all. "That's fascinating, man. You say that this Celebration of Life is going on now. And Rotart says it possible for us to attend?"

"Yes," replied Omar as they walked to the shuttles. "The Celebration of Life goes on for a full week but on the final night, tomorrow all of the people from every village, town and city assemble at the rivers and lakes for the Festival of Lights where they pay tribute and say goodbye to those who have traveled to the beyond in the past year. Their candles are lit one final time before being placed in front of the chamber that contains their remains. We must go to the power plant now. You will not encounter many workers. They would have already left for the shoreline to paint and decorate their boats for the contest. I will speak more of this later." All of Earth's leaders were very impressed with what they saw. The air, the water, even the soil was clean.

Later in the day when the sky began to turn reddish orange. The group was taken to the Whistling Forest. Omar explained to the group that the forest got is name from the sounds made by the leaves when the wind passes through them. "You see ladies and gentlemen. We are very near the ocean and Lazon was designed to have a constant three to four mile per hour breeze twenty eight hours a day. It is the tiny holes in the leaves that will make a low whistling sound; our people find it quite tranquil and peaceful, often leaving one feeling docile. As I have stated before, they help to keep our eco-system in balance. Here you will also notice thousands of oxyflox plants. Please do not pick the flowers. It is forbidden. We have prepared a lavish dinner for you here in this beautiful setting. I must leave for now. Let me introduce Katjarogen my assistant. She will answer your questions until my return." Katjarogen was different from the other females she was short and slender with dark hair and eyes. She spoke in almost a whisper. She led the group into a clearing in the forest. Large Amish like quilts were laid out with many different types of fruits and vegetables that Walker did not recognize. Katajorgen encouraged them to sit. As she began passing around the beverages a bearded gentleman asked if the beverages contained alcohol. "It is against our religion," replied Katjairogen. "And please it is just Katja, all of my friends call me Katja." President Walker seemed lost in the moment. He thought to himself. *Will it be possible for people of New Earth to live this good? No poverty or pollution, unlimited energy.* Walker laid back on the quilt and listened to the trees. They sounded like they were singing. This is the closest to paradise that I have come to. He didn't want leave the intoxicating, peaceful forest. Upon leaving the forest, everyone could not help but notice that the mother ship had arrived and landed atop the ridge overlooking the forest. Katja clapped her hands.

"Everyone, please gather around. Tonight at 11:45, you are invited to the ship's observation deck to view the whistling forest during rainfall. The rain will begin at exactly 11:45, so do not be late." The British Prime Minister attempted to correct her with out seeming rude. "Ah, Katja, what happens if it does not rain?" She laughed, and in her most reassuring voice said. "Oh, there will be rain and it will start at 11:45 and end at 1:45. You must remember, sir. This is Lazon. We do not predict when it will rain we control it with our environmentorizors just as we do the air pollution. The clouds are seeded with moisture and heated to the optimum temperature at the proper time. It is very complex. I do not claim to understand the process, but I can assure you that it has never failed." When they returned to the ship Walker waited for Fantana to walk him back to his room. Instead, Katja approached him. "I will escort you Mr. President." Walker looked disappointed. "What happened to Fantana?" He asked. "Fantana has left the service of Rotart and this vessel. She will not be returning I have been assigned to replace her. Is there a problem?" "No. Not at all." The news snapped Walker back into reality. He remembered the warning that Fantana had given him. Walker suspected foul play. Suddenly, a wave of guilt and vulnerability washed over him. He realized that interrogation was the least of his problems. He could turn up missing just like Fantana.

Walker grabbed the pouch and took it to his closest ally on the ship. The Prime Minister of Britain. He spent hours telling the Prime Minister what he knew and together they read the book given to him by Fantana. The chimes sounded on the ships P.A system. It was Katja. "The time is 11:30. All interested parties who wish to view the forest must summon their escorts now." Walker looked at the speaker then to the Prime Minister. "I should go. Look, if anything happens to me come to my quarters and find this book. I keep it in the bottom of my suitcase. This has all the proof you need to put this S.O.B out of business. Can I count on you?" The Prime Minister shook Walker's hand. "You know you can, man."

The entire ship including the crew members and Omar assembled on the observation deck staring into night at the dark forest. "Omar looked at his watch eleven forty five," he said. The first raindrops began to fall. Katja stood to the left of Walker and the Prime Minster to his right she leaned forward just enough to see the look on the Minster's face when the rain started to fall. Suddenly, a small blue light glowed through the darkness, then red, and green. Before you knew it, the entire forest was a wash in flickering lights of all shapes and colors, each glowing brightly and fading. Hundreds of lights just like Christmas. The group cheered and clapped in approval. "What is it?" someone asked "What is the source of the lights?" Omar turned to the crowd. "It is the rocks. This phenomenon happened quite by accident. When this planet was terra-formed, the composition of the minerals in some of the rocks combined with the pollen from the oxyflox and after years of using the economist spray they have produced this wonderful array of lights. It is totally harmless. Lovers often visit here to propose. Keep watch." Omar instructed. "Look, over there." Omar pointed to the open area of the forest where they had dined earlier in the day. At the forest edge an animal appeared and then another. "Horses," Walker cried. "No," said Katja. "Look closely Unicorns." She handed Walker a pair of night vision binocular. "Well I'll be," said Walker. "You're right. There must be six or seven of them." He passed the binoculars to the Prime Minister. Katja continued. "Actually, there are several hundred. This is a protected planet. Animals especially Unicorns are not allowed to be harmed. They love the lights. Just look at them. Magnificent aren't they?" Everyone marveled at what they saw. Even in Rotart's absence he was still slowly drawing them in. Omar left but returned before the light show ended. "Great news!" He said with a wide grin. "Rotart has managed to acquire enough boats for us to attend tomorrow night's Festival Of Lights. Cheers came from the crowd." Walker looked at the Prime Minister. It appears that Rotart's charade would continue for at least another day.

Walker and the Prime Minster walked to the far side of the deck to talk in private. The Prime Minister gazed at the colorful light show as he talked. "I am afraid we are losing the battle my friend. That Rotart is the craftiest bugger I have ever seen. Today in the forest, that was the deal closer. Did you see their faces? He has singing trees, exotic birds, butterflies and a soft warm breeze. Utopia, Nirvana, Xanadu, call it what you like. Today was the seduction. Tonight, well, tonight was the icing on the cake." Walker swirled his drink round and round as he nodded in agreement. "Yea," Walker agreed "But can you blame them? He is offering them the answer to all of our problems but only we know that he can't deliver. There's only three or four left on the fence. If tomorrow's boat show is anything like today's little picnic in the park." "Well," Walker paused then took a sip of the blue liquid in his glass. "We can pack it in old friend. We will have to try to undo all this when we get home." The Prime Minster looked around to be sure no one was around before he spoke. "It all comes down to the book. Without it you can stick a fork in us cause we are done."

After breakfast, the group of leaders were led back to the observation deck. Overnight, the ship traveled to the other side of the planet and now hovered over a large ocean. Once again, Rotart managed to impress the group. It was an amazing site. The water was crystal clear and filled with thousands of boats. Omar allowed everyone to soak up the atmosphere before giving one of his now familiar speeches. "Good morning, everyone. Welcome to the Festival of Life. What you see before you is a tradition that goes back thousands of years. There are boats of every size, type and design from all across the galaxy but they all have one thing in common. They are constructed with wood. With the exception of the power supply, eighty-five percent of the watercrafts must be wooded to qualify in the judgment. Each year the High Rullers of each area award prizes for the best boats. Some families take the competition quite seriously. Not because of the prizes. It's considered an honor, a matter of pride." The Spanish leader was taken aback watching as the high-tech spaceships were lowering extremely low-tech boats down into the water. "After all these years," he remarked, they have not abandoned their heritage or customs. With a wave of his arm across the sea of boats, Omar gave everyone the lowdown. "Each family member over the age of five participates in the decoration of the boat, the preparation of the food, even the selection of music. The candles are placed in colorful vases or globes and placed in prominate positions on the vessel. The white candle, the candle of the deceased is placed on the bow of the boat." Katja entered the deck and whispered into Omar's ear. "Thank you, Katja. Ladies and gentlemen, if you will follow me I will take you to the boats so that we can be lowered down and clear the air space for other ships." Through the day the captain maneuvered the boat around the other vessels on the water so that Walker and the other nine leaders with him could watch the families taking care of last minute touch up's of painting or food preparation. Katja and Prime Minster Major were in Walker's Party. Katja called Walker's attention to the fish. "President Walker, have you noticed the sea life?" "Yes, I have. But I am more impressed with the clarity of your water. It must me at least a hundred feet down and I can still see the bottom." While Walker was looking down the Prime Minster was looking up. "Katja, why are there so many flags?" "Ah, yes she nodded. Identification, not all family members arrive at once. The flags are used to distinguish each ship from a distance."

As night fell, Walker could smell the aroma wafting over from the ships surrounding theirs. People began gathering along the shoreline in large numbers. Walker sat alone near the rear of the boat until Katja came over to join him. "Mr. President is everything all right?" "Yes, well. I was wondering, if this is a festival why is there no singing or dancing? There is no music and no eating." Haven't you noticed?" Katja looked to the sky. "One hour before midnight." She gently placed her hand on his knee. "Patience it will not be long now." Omar gathered the group to one side of the boat just before thirteen o'clock. He pointed to the shore. Suddenly everything went black. Every light on every ship went dark. The shore was no longer visible because there was no light. Then one by one, lights began to flicker but this time was different. Omar explained in a whisper. "The only lights you will see for the next hour are the candle flames lit one final time. These are the candles of those who have gone before us. Tomorrow, they will be placed at the feet of the owner in the chamber at the City of the Lost. The ceremony is held on water because water represents life. You may use this time to pray or meditate if you wish but we must remain absolutely silent to honor those who have gone before us." President Walker watched the white candles on the boats closest to his. He tried to keep quiet but his stomach would not cooperate. The last time he had eaten was more than ten hours ago. He tried to imagine the billions of candles that would be needed if he and the Prime Minister failed at their task of warning the other nations before it was too late.

The hour passed quickly. A loud gong followed by a bright flare lit up the night sky that startled Walker. The next faze of the festival had begun. Walker and his party watched as the family elders lowered the candles into the river using string then placed them in a sliver box. Almost like magic colorful lights, globes, and clothing were everywhere. The sound of music and the smell of delicious food filled the air. Walker did not recognize any of the instruments or the food but it didn't seem to matter. Enormous bon fires dotted the rivers edge. The golden embers drifted high into the night sky like thousands of fireflies floating on air. The vibrant colors painted on the sides of the boats gave off reflections that seem to dance atop the water. Children barely old enough to walk were singing and dancing right along with their parents and grandparents. The Prime Minister walked continuously from one side of the boat with the others taking in as much as they could. With a drink in one hand and a plate stacked with food in the other he nearly collided with Walker. "Amazing isn't it?" Said the Prime Minister. "I don't know if it's the contrast between life and death or something else entirely but I will tell you one thing Walker. These people have a real appreciation of life." The party continued till dawn. The food was plentiful and delicious. The music, singing, and dancing on the boats and on shore was non-stop. Omar called for the ship at first light and it was over. Rotart was there to greet the party goes when they returned to the ship.

After dinner, he asked Walker to accompany him to his quarters so that they could speak in private. Rotart's accommodations were far more lavish than any Walker had ever seen. Royal blues and gold filled the room. Everything from ceiling to carpets was rich in color. "President Walker I will get right to the point. Inside this book are the signatures of all but five of the world's leaders. Most of those aboard this ship signed this morning. Canada, Italy, the United Kingdom and Mexico are pending. They will only sign if you do." Rotart put the book on the desk and slowly slid it over to Walker. "Time is running out. The others have requested that we return to Earth so that they can get started, I have honored that request." Rotart handed Walker the pen. "Do what is best for your people, for your planet. Sign the document and enjoy your trip home." Walker took the pen and laid it on the desk. "I must respectfully decline," said Walker. "You have been a great host, and a generous host, but I have to play this out. The risk is just too great." Rotart held back his anger. "Very well, maybe I can convince you before we reach Earth."

The trip home seems faster than the trip to Lazon. On the final night Rotart threw a huge feast complete with music and dancers. Once again, Walker found himself back in Rotart's quarters. Rotart began to pace from one side of the desk to the other. "President Walker, I have, as you Americans are fond of saying sweetened the deal. As we speak our scientist are working on modifying our enviormentorlizers to function on Earth. Let me be more specific. In one year thirty-eight enviormentolozers can be cleaning the air over the United States night and day. Now sign!" Rotart practically forced the pen into Walker's hand. "No sale," said Walker. It was clear that the tone of their meeting was considerably more hostile then the last meeting. Rotart produced a second document. "Since you are determined to abandon your planet, I have taken the liberty of drawing up a new contract. An entire planet of four or five countries is such a waste. This will give you and other four countries the rights to twenty-five percent of the New Earth. Far more than you will ever need." Walker stared at Rotart long and hard. "We were promised the entire planet. Why settle for less? Your contracts are as transparent as glass and as useless as a car with two wheels. We both know what's going on here, so lets'cut the crap shall we. Game over. You lose." Walker threw the pen to the floor and went back to the party.

The next morning when he got up to pack President Walker could hardly walk. Katja took him to the infirmary but the ship's psychical doctor was baffled. "I am not familiar with the human anatomy." he explained. "Although, our appearance is similar on the outside there are many differences on the inside." When the Prime Minister heard the news, he rushed to the infirmary to try to help his friend. Walker was growing weaker. When the men were alone Walker told the Prime Minister what had happened. "Go to my room and get the book." he said. The Prime Minister looked worried. "Hang in there buddy. In a few hours we will be home." "The book," Walker whispered. "Go get the book." The Prime Minister entered the room and was immediately hit over the back of the head by a thief laying in wait. When the Prime Minister came to only the pouch laid on the floor next to him but the book was long gone. Rotart's ship made a detour to drop President Walker off at the White House.

Walker's condition was deteriorating rapidly. Two of Rotart's aides had to carry him off the ship on a stretcher. The Prime Minster's from Spain and England accompanied Walker into the White House while Rotart continued on to New York. Rotart stood on the steps of the United Nations and re-affirmed his commitment to return in exactly one year. There was no mention of President Walker in his speech. After his speech, he posed with various Chancellors, President's and other world leaders before leaving. Back at the White House everyone was in scramble mode. The President was rushed directly to the hospital. The British Prime Minister briefed the Vice President on what had gone on during the last few days. "I believe your President was poisoned." said the Prime Minster Eric was stunned. He knew he had no time to waste. He called the hospital and insisted that the top toxic specialist be brought in ASAP. Eric turned back to the Prime Minster. "How could this happen? What would Rotart gain by poisoning President Walker?" The Prime Minster seemed surprised by Eric's questions. "The answers are as plain as the nose on your face man. Rotart knew that Walker was about to expose him. Rotart knew about the book maybe he thought Walker had more proof. Rotart was running scared, he is quite desperate. He sees Walker as a threat. Without his opposition, those on the fence would come over to his side. You should have been there. He can be very persuasive. I have to admit for a while he almost had me fooled." Just then, a young woman entered the room. "Mr. Vice President your car is ready to take you to the Bethesda." Eric and the Prime Minster entered the President's room just as the sheet was being draped over Walker's face. President Walker had died..

CHAPTER 15

▼

REALITY CHECK

News of the President's death spread quickly. Late that night a steady stream of black limos could be seen entering the gates of the White House. The Chief Justice of the Supreme Court arrived to swear in, the soon to be President, Eric Thompson in a hastily arranged ceremony in the White House West Wing. Eric gestured to Mrs. Robinson. "Mrs. Robinson, may I speak to you for a moment in private?" Without waiting for her to answer, Eric whisked her off into the anti-room. Her eyes were red from crying. Mrs. Robinson was more to President Walker than an assistant, she was his friend. Walker often referred to her as the rock. "I know that this is a difficult time for you and I really hate to put you in this position but I need you to continue on with me as you did for President Walker. You were his right hand and he valued your service, as do I." Mrs. Robinson patted Eric on the hand. She managed to hold back the tears when she spoke. "Eric, I would not dream of abandoning you at a time like this. Of course, I'll stay." "Thank you, Mrs. Robinson. That means a lot to me." "Well, Mr. President, your staff is waiting for you and members of the House and Senate are starting to arrive. There is much to be done tonight. Shall we get started?"

Will, Art and Matt were miles away from the White House when Eric was sworn in. The British Prime Minster Anthony Major requested a meeting with the trio. It was 3:20 in the morning when they arrived at the British Embassy. "Gentlemen, thank you for coming. Please have a seat. I owe you an explanation for all the cloak and dagger business. You see, President Walker and I have developed a very close friendship during our trip to Lazon." Matt was about to interrupt when the Prime Minister anticipated his question. "I know what you are thinking Matt. There was a change of plans. We never made it to Otar. I have asked you here so that we could speak in private. No one knows that this meeting is taking place and for good reason. The world owes you three a debt that we could never repay. While Walker was away he managed to piece together everything from your meetings with the aliens to Rotart's plot to hijack our new home planet." Will, Eric and Matt looked at each other but kept quiet. "That's right guys he knew it all and he passed that knowledge on to me. You can relax. Your secret is safe with me. When he took ill, he asked me to thank you all, especially Matt for sticking to your guns. He said, "Now, I understand." Let me tell you the whole story."

Just as Prime Minister Major finished he received a phone call. "Hello, yes. What? Bloody hell, what nerve! Cheeky bastard! No, I won't be going to Downing Street. Yes, straightaway, okay, keep in touch. Good-bye." The Prime Minister was furious. Art walked over to the desk where he was standing. He was muttering under his breath. Art spoke in his most respectful tone. "Sir, are you okay?" "I bloody will be when I have Rotart's head on a stick. Our government has agreed to allow this fraud this charlatan to speak to the House of Commons tomorrow. My plane won't be here for another three hours. What's he up to? He knows I would not be there. He's a crafty one, murdered Walker cause he knew too much. Made it look like an accident but, he could not get rid of me. Art do you still have family in England?" "Yes sir, I do. A few relatives and my wife's people as well." "Well Arthur, why don't you fly back with me? I could use the company." Art stroked his chin. "That's a very generous offer sir. My grand's in poor health and I would like to pop in for a visit." Art turned to Will and Matt. "But what about Eric and the funeral? I may be needed here." Will flagged him off. "Naw man, Matt and I can handle things on this side of the pond. Go." "Yea," said Matt. The Prime Minister seemed calmer now. He patted Art on the back. "You are fortunate to have such good mates. You should take their advice. Maybe we could put our heads together and get rid of this Rotart scum once and for all." President Walker's body will lie in state for at least three days. "I will be returning for the funeral. You can ride back with me. So it's settled." The Prime Minister shook Matt and Will's hands and thanked them again. "Minister, one last question." "Yes, Will. What's on your mind?" "Well, sir, President Thompson is a good man and a friend. He's bound to find out about this meeting eventually. What should we tell him?" "Well son, the truth is always the best policy. I mean tell him we met and why. But I would advise all of you to keep the details between us in order to protect him. Don't ever forget that it was Walker's burning curiosity that got him killed. Keep your cards close to your vest at all times lads."

When the Prime Minster and Art arrived at the House of Commons Rotart had come and gone but the members were waiting to vote yes or no on Rotart's new proposal. Without the Prime Minister it was an easy sell. The green leather benches were packed to the rafters. A portly man in the third row addressed the Prime Minister. "We have been offered the technology to control our weather. This will be a major boast to our economy. It would be a tremendous asset to our farmers. This is an addition to Rotart's original offer." "It would be irresponsible to accept that deal!" Yelled, Art. "Not only that, it would be suicidal." The crowd jeered and moaned. They were all for passage of the offer. The Prime Minster called for calm. He introduced Arthur as a liaison on loan from America. A gentleman about thirty-ish took the floor. "With all due respect, to the late President Walker, the last time we took the advice of the American's was the fiasco in the Middle East. American's have no say in these walls." "I agree" said Art. "American's do not." "Here, here." said the group of mostly middle aged men. "Nevertheless, I do." Art spoke in the most authoritative voice he could muster. "My loyalty is to Queen and country. I was born and raised on British soil." More groans came from the green stands. An elderly man wearing a gray suit used his cane to help lift him from his seat. He seemed upset with the other members. "Let him speak!" Shouted the man.

The room fell silent. Art walked over to where the Prime Minster stood. Art thanked the old man and began again. "Ask yourselves, would you give a stranger money to purchase an item before having a chance to see the merchandise? No, you would not. Disabling our ships, our only means of surviving the coming devastation would doom us all. If Rotart does not return and we are stranded you can expect, bus size chunks of what's left of the rouge planet Teldran to slam into Earth at a high velocities. Many of these humongous boulders will be fireballs. It will scorch the Earth with fire and heat the ocean waters up to 233 degrees and that's just the beginning. A large portion of that charging planet will remain intact crashing into the Atlantic Ocean causing a duo tsunami of epic proportions. According to computer models, twin waves of over four hundred and sixty feet will hit England from the west and put out the fires while drowning perhaps millions in the process." Art paused for effect as he looked at the faces around the Great Hall. "The bad news is that every living thing in its path will be boiled alive." People were gasping and murmuring at Art spoke. He held up his hand for quiet. "When the flames are out and the waters have subsided those who survived will experience the equivalent of a nuclear winter. The Earth will be knocked off its axis. Day and night, summer and winter, rain and snow, as we know it will never be the same. In short, farmers will no longer have the ability to grow crops. Those who survived will soon wish that they didn't. The fates of millions of British citizens are in your hands! The choice is a simple one: Life or death. I choose to live. That is why I will be aboard Space Craft One leaving from the White House in December 2012. If you choose unwisely, my prayers will be with you."

Art did not field any questions but fearing the worst he went straight to the limo and waited quietly in the back seat for the Prime Minister to return. His hands were shaking. Art thought to himself. *I have just talked to the most powerful group of men and women in all of England. What was I thinking? Why would they listen to me a computer geek?* It wasn't long before the Prime Minster joined him. "Ah, George, take us to Number 10 please." The driver tipped his hat and drove off. The Prime Minister slapped Art on the knee. "That was bloody brilliant, Art. Hell of a speech. Could not have done it without you, the vote against Rotart was unanimous. Not a dry eye in the House. I am recommending you for knighthood. That's the very least that I could do." Art was dumbfounded. He did not expect any of this. He came to visit his grand and ended up saving all of England. Not a bad day at all.

Art returned to Washington in time for the funeral. President Thompson called for a meeting with Will, Sara, Art and Matt. When they arrived, Mrs. Robinson was there writing something on a pad. Walker had just been laid to rest and no one was in the mood for a meeting but there was work to be done. Eric entered the room and glanced at his watch before taking a seat next to Mrs. Robinson. "Sorry I'm late. Let's get down to business," he said. "First thing's first. Art, I have not had a chance to congratulate your handling of the problem with our British friends last week. Hell of a job." The President pumped his fist in the air. "The Prime Minster has formally requested that you be on call as the official liaison between the United States and the Brit's until the end of this crisis. Will, I know this is not your area but I am removing the head of the Ark project. I want you to oversee the retro fitting and completion of both Ark's east and west coast. He's had two years and he's just not getting it done. Sara, I understand that you are a head of schedule on the *hydroponics* gardens and food supply. Listen those people who have decided to stay are going to need to eat. Can you and your people set up a similar program using the ships gardening technology to teach these folks how to grow crops underground?" Sara was intrigued by the idea. "Why yes Eric, I mean Mr. President, I believe I can. That's a fantastic idea." President Thompson closed the note pad in front of him. "Excellent, I will set up a meeting with them later in the week. Art, contact the British Embassy. The Ambassador will brief you. Will, you need to contact this man." Eric handed Will a business card. "Sara start with the bottom dwellers at the Sanctuary location. Thank you all for coming." Eric smiled turned and left the room.

Something was wrong and everyone noticed it. Eric did not acknowledge Matt's presence at the meeting. It was as if he was not there. Will turned to Art. "What was that all about?" Will wondered. Art shrugged his shoulders. Matt was hurt. You could see it in his eyes and hear it in his voice. Matt tried his best to offer an explanation. "He's been this way since Walker's death. But why take it out on me? I thought we were friends." "So did he," Mrs. Robinson interjected. "At least he did until he found out about your little secret meeting with the Prime Minster." Matt leaned forward. "He knows!" "Oh yeah," replied Mrs. Walker. "Found out last night." Sara jabbed Matt in the ribs with her elbow. "I thought you were going to tell him." Matt nodded. "I was, I never got around to it. Everything's been so crazy around here." Sara stared directly at Matt. He knew what that look meant. She wasn't buying any of it. "Matt you need to go and fix this right now! Go!" Matt looked to Will for support, but Will also knew the look and decided to let Matt fend for himself. Matt knew Eric did not smoke but his father did. Matt used his Cuban connections to buy a box of their finest cigars. He also sent Eric a case of Dark Jamaican Rum. Eric accepted the peace offering. His dad was happy to receive the cigars. After one very long explaination, several apologies, and a half bottle of Rum Matt and Eric were good friends again.

Nearly a year had gone by merchants everywhere were beginning to sell countdown clocks and other kinds of end of the world memorabilia. Everywhere you looked the flasing red numbers were a constant reminder of what was to come. After Walker death several countries decided to back out of the deal with Rotart. The ones that had put their faith in Rotart and the Otarians were waiting for his return. On the eve of the Equinox, Matt was a nervous wreck he knew that Rotart would not return as promised. Millions of lives hung in the balance and there was not much that he could do. Matt knew how sensitive Sara was and he realized that he had to be strong for her sake. On the day of the Autumnal Equinox, the crowds were much smaller than a year ago. Most of the countries that rejected Rotart's offer did not bother to send a representative, but the media was in full force. Sara looked at Matt. "Honey, it's time, right?" "Yes, Sara it's time alright." Sara looked at her husband. "They aren't coming, are they?" "No babe, I am afraid not." After three hours of waiting on the United Nation steps, the chill in the September air had begun to take its toll. Germany, France, Russia and a dozen smaller countries were screwed and the whole world knew it. The Secretary

General of the UN called its members inside for a late night emergency session. "May I have your attention please?" The secretary spoke into the microphone. "As you are aware, we have already decided on a contingency plan in the event that the aliens did not show. The plan is to construct large underground shelters to give whatever protection and aid we can to the countries who will be left behind. This is most unfortunate but it is no longer feasible to construct enough new ships to replace those that has been permanently secured and are no longer worthy of space travel."

Most of the leaders were too stunned to talk. A few looked as if they had been kicked in the gut. One man wept openly. The dye had been cast and the fate of their fellow citizens had been sealed. "We are rapidly running out of time. Therefore, we will be asking the world communities to donate money for heavey equipment such as bulldozers, dump trucks, plows, earthmovers and other machinery."

The secretary general noticed that only a few hands were raised. He pointed to the representative from Spain. "Spain pledges thirty million dollars." Next was the Swiss President, "We pledge twenty one million," and so it went. For thirty minutes the pledges came rolling in until President Thompson spoke. "Mr. Secretary, The United States of America pledges ten." "The United States of America pledges ten million dollars." said the Secretary General. "Mr. President the United States of America is a very wealthy country surely you can be more generous than ten million dollars." President Thompson laughed. "Mr. Secretary General, with all due respect what you are offering is false hope. A bandage. In the end these people will die. We, the United States of America offer LIFE!. I am not here to offer money. I am offering ships. Ten ships a year for the remaining three years." The crowd burst into thunderous applause. Everyone in the auditorium rose to their feet. The event was carried live on C-Span. As expected Sara was deeply depressed until she heard the President's offer. She leaped off the bed and screamed. She gave Matt a big hug. "You knew didn't you? You knew and you never said a word." Tears of joy streamed down Sara's face. Matt grinned at his wife. "I was sworn to secrecy by Eric. We started building extra ships in the Arizona desert right after Eric became President. He wanted to keep things hush-hush incase Rotart did come back. Watch the TV. There's more."

After the applause died down, Eric continued. "Who will join me in offering life?" British Prime Minister Major rose from his seat. "The UK will stand with the US and match its offer of ten ships for three years." Sara gave Matt a shove. "You," she said. "You could have told me. What other countries are in on this?" "Just us two," said Matt. "Wait keep watching." Soon country after country began joining the cause. Matt changed the channel. Earlier there was rioting in the streets in various countries who had given up their ships believing in Rotart's return. By the time the meeting was over two hundred and ten ships were pledged to be built and safe passage and access given to countries without ships. Once the news got out the riots stopped, but the victory would not completely solve the problem. Lives would be saved but Matt knew that at the end of the day millions would still be left behind.

CHAPTER 16

▼

A LAND DOWN UNDER

Matt had grown accustomed to the nightly dreams of the planet Lazon but he had no inkling of what lied ahead for him and his friends. It was 3:37 in the morning when he first realized that something was up. Matt sat on the side of the bed trying to recall the image from the dream he just had when Sara rolled over to the warm spot in the bed where Matt had laid just a few moments ago. "What's the matter Matt?" Sara's words were slurred. She sounded like she had been drinking. Matt rubbed her back. "Nothing babe, go back to sleep." Matt sat down at the desk on the other side of the room and drew a sketch of the image from his dream as best as he could remember it. After he was satisfied with the drawing, he slid it under the blotter and went back to bed.

Three days later right in the middle of the guy's weekly Pinochle game another image flashed into Matt's head. He turned to Eric. "I need a pen and paper. Now. Please." Matt said urgently. Eric looked puzzled. "Can't it wait till the end of the hand?" "No!" Said Matt. "It can't." The men around the table were equally puzzled but let Eric handle things. Minutes latter Matt sketched out another image on the paper that Eric handed to him. The large bearded man sitting next to Matt leaned forward to check out the picture. "OK Picasso, what is it?" "I don't know," Matt was calmer now. "I don't usually get these images during the day. This is starting to freak me out." Eric didn't want to say too much with the other men listening. He took a quick look and handed it back to Matt. "Let's run it through the computer tomorrow and see what we come up with," he said. "Bring the rest with you."

The next morning, the super computer summed up the images in two words. Insufficient data. Matt's visions continued for weeks. A worried Sara urged Matt to discuss it with Will and Art but Matt politely refused. "Listen Sara, people around here already think that I am going off my rocker. It's bad enough that I had to drag Eric into this. I am not going drag Art and Will into this madness. Wait till I have something more concrete. I'm going to play cards, see you in a bit." He gave Sara a peck on the lips and was out the door. An hour later, Will and Art were sitting in Sara's living room having drinks. "I am really sorry guys. I know that this is last minute but I just feel like the situation is really spiraling out of control and I don't know who else to turn too." Will sat his drink down on the coaster. "It's going to be all right Sara, Art and I are here to help anyway we can. Tell us what's going on. Just spit it out." Sara walked over to the desk and produced the napkin that Matt was saving in the top drawer. She handed it to Will. "This is what Matt drew when we were at dinner last week," she began to explain. Then she pulled out a photograph from here purse. "He drew this one on the bathroom mirror in the middle of the night using my eyebrow pencil. He would not let me clean the mirror until he took that picture." Will studied the napkin and the photo before handing them to Art. "What's it supposed to be?," asked Art. "Neither of us have the faintest idea," she said. "But this has been going on for almost a month." "A month!" cried Art. "How many of these drawings does he have?" "I don't know," Sara shrugged her shoulders. She thought for a minute and turned to Art. "Wait!" She went into the bedroom and returned with a rather large sketchpad. "After the bathroom mirror incident, I gave him this. He keeps it under the bed and it keeps him out of my makeup." Will shook his head as he flipped through the images. "Are you telling us that he gets these images 24/7? That must be rough on your sex life." Sara gave Will a look of frustration. "Don't even get me started, Will. You don't know the half of it." Art was busy studying the impressions on the pad. "All right you two can we please focus on the real problem here? All I see is random symbols and clusters. There must be about 70 different drawings."

"Seventy-seven to be exact," said Matt. Matt surprised everyone by returning home earlier than usual. No one noticed him standing in the doorway. He looked straight at Sara. "You just could not leave it alone, could you?" "Don't blame her," said Art. "I thought we were in this thing together. I thought that we were a team. You should have confided in us." Matt was on the defensive. "I tried too," he explained. "When the images first started me and Eric wanted to bring you guys in but you were out of town. Anyway, two days ago the images stopped coming." Will took the pad out of Arts hands and stared waving it at Matt. "Two days ago," said Will "And you still didn't call us. This is probably very important, Matt. Just what the hell were you thinking?" Matt searched for the right words but there weren't any. He rubbed his hands together and decided that it was best to face the music. *Three against one*, he thought. He was wrong and he knew it. "Okay, everybody look, the three of you can stand there all night and beat up on me for being a jerk, or we can finally find out what all of this means."

Art worked through the night carefully entering all of the data into the same super computer that was used to interpret the original crop circle pictures. With Will helping out they were able to finish by early morning. When they returned to Matt's place, Art looked like the cat that swallowed the canary. "Gather round boys and girls." Art waved his hands like the a carnival barker. He opened his laptop and began to explain what happened. "Will and I ran the same program as before but this time something weird happened. The computer began searching all the files connected to the crop circles and pulled specific bits of data from most of the files. This, my friends, is the result." Art tapped a few more keys and spun the laptop around so that everyone could see. "It's a ship." cried Sara. "A ship with a complete set of blueprints," said Will. "They call it the Sprite." Art pointed to the screen. "It's really quite small," he said. "Could probably fit into this room. This had to come from T'Zar. I guess this means that someone's going to take a trip." "Why?," said Matt. "Why would Onan and T'zar want us to build another ship?" Will stroked his chin while he pondered Matt's question. "I don't know, buddy." "You know how it's been going. You solve one mystery and up pops another. Maybe they have been found out. Maybe Earth is not going to be saved and they are sending us this ship so that we can get out. Why are you asking us? You are supposed to be the one with all the answers." "Well you guys, let's do it. Let's get Eric on the horn so that we can get this show on the road."

The Sprite was built in secret, at Area 51 to keep it away from prying eyes. It was completed in just under a month. One week after it's construction the President met with Art, Will, and Matt. "I am sending you three to Area 51." Will held his head low. "Not again," he muttered under his breath. Eric updated the men on the lack of progress on the Sprite. "The tech guys cannot get the ship to operate at all. They can't even get the lights to work. You guys are our only hope." Art took a step forward. "Wait Mr. President, we aren't technicians. We don't know a bloody thing about space ships." Eric tried to reason with them.

"Look Art, you guys are all I have. You've gotten us this far. Humor me. Just fly out there and take a look at it. Okay?"

When the men reached Area 51 later that day, they were escorted to a large hanger on the far side of the base. Everything from the walls to the windows and ceilings were painted battleship grey on the inside and a sandy brown on the outside. In the center of the room, was the mysterious new space ship constructed from Matt's visions. The Sprite was not a pretty ship in fact it looked downright dull. It was the color of a nickel that was left in a kid's piggy bank for a few years. Will, Matt, and Art were led over to four men with clipboards wearing long white lab coats. Will extended his hand. "Hi, I'm Will, who does your decorating around here?" The technicians were not amused. If fact they seamed almost hostile. They made it clear that Matt and the others were not welcomed. There was an air of smugness and a condescending tone in their voice. The older of the technicians seemed to be the spokes person for the four. "I am afraid that you have come all this way for nothing," he said. "I don't see anything that you can do that we have not already tried. We have decided that the schematics that you sent were incorrect." Will took exception to his tone. "Look fellows, why don't you loose the attitude. We just came here to have a look around." One of the men handed Will a flashlight. "Be my guest," he said. The door was open and the tiny ship was pitch black inside. Art was the first to enter the vessel. He shinned the light onto the console then to the view screen and over to the seats. The seats formed a V shape, two in the front and one in the back. Will entered behind Art and Matt brought up the rear. The second that Matt set foot on the craft all of the ships lights came on. This really surprised the technicians. They rushed aboard the ship to get a look around but as soon as they crossed the threshold, the lights went out again. This happened each time they tried to enter until they finally accepted the fact that this ride was by invitation only and that Matt, Art, and Will were the only invited guests.

With the lab guys out of the way, Matt and the others were finally able to take a look around. "Not much to see," said Matt. "A view screen, couple of storage bins, bathroom, and a computer that we have absolutely no idea how to operate." Art sat down in one of the gray high back chairs. "Hey guys," he called out. "Check this out." A small flat panel began to emerge from the right side of Art's chair. "Blimey. It's got a hand imprint on it. Well, here goes." He gingerly placed his hand on the plate. "Nothing," he whispered. Will and Matt decided to follow Art's lead. When they all simultaneously put their hands on the three plates, the ship began to hum. You could even feel a slight vibration from the ships floor. "What's that!" yelled Matt. The men kept their hands in place. "I think it's the ships engines," said Will. "I think it's powering up." Before long the ships life support systems, the computers, the view screen, everything aboard the ship sprang to life for the first time. Matt jerked his hand off the plate. "This is just not natural. How did they know?" Even with Matt's hand off the control plate the little Sprite continued to function. Art and Will followed suit, but the ships computer still remained operational. "Matt! Art! Come and check this out." Will had discovered a small black countdown clock with red numbers just like the ones on the larger ships being built for the evacuation. "Look familiar?", he said. Matt pointed at the glowing numbers. "Not good boys. He shook his head. Days, not years or months," said Art. "This ship is going to leave in seven days four hours and nine minutes." Matt rubbed his hands through his hair as he turned away from the clock. "This is nuts. What are the Guardians thinking? What do they want us to do?" "Seems pretty clear to me," said Will. "They expect us to be on this ship when it takes off next week." Matt spun around to face Will and Art. It was clear that he was more than a little nervous. "Yea!" he shouted. "Board a ship that we don't know how to fly and go to where? Huh, Just where are they sending us and why haven't they come to tell us in person? This is total B.S."

The President debated the pros and cons of taking the trip with Matt, Will, and Art right up till the last hours before the flight. The final decision was left up to them. With less than three hours to go everyone (some more reluctantly than others) decided that it could be a fatal mistake for the threesome to abort the mission. Art, Matt, and Will strapped themselves in as they watched the ships door slide shut. Art took a deep breath. "Well, I guess this is it then. Let's see what happens." They could feel the ship slowly rise from the floor toward the large hanger doors that where already open overhead. "Just as I figured," said Art. "Everything is on auto command." Will checked his watch. 12:30. "Man, these guys sure are punctual." The reluctant travelers still did not know where they were going, or when they would arrive. Nevertheless, the biggest question on everyone's mind is if they would ever return to Earth.

The ship quickly headed for the heavens and through the Astral Corridor before long, it was speeding through constellations of Lacerta, Andromeda, and Perseus. For six and a half hours, the men hardly spoke as they watched the little ship zoom into the Flash Lanes and onward to deep space. Without warning, the Sprite drifted to a stop and hovered over the Red planet. "Mars," whispered Art. "It has to be the planet Mars." Will shook his head. "No way," he said to Art "Can't be. We haven't been gone for more than seven hours tops." The sprite started downward toward the surface but did not attempt to land. As the ship made its decent two large, sandy red doors opened on the planets surface. The ship dropped droped down through the open doors and continued lower and lower beneath the planet's surface. Once they passed through the doors above them closed but there were dim yellow lights on the cavern walls surrounding the ship. When they finally reached a clearing Matt could not believe what he was watching on the view screen. Ships of all shapes and sizes were landing and taking off from below. "Take a look guys. Looks like some kinda underground spaceport." The Sprite maneuvered through the maze of ships and touched down in an isolated corner next to what looked like a large freighter.

The doors of the Sprite gently slide open to what looked like an abandoned area of the port. Will nervously rubbed his hands together as he peeped through the opened doors. "Well guys. This looks like our stop. Let us do it." As they made their exit, Art noticed three women walking down the ramp from the freighter. They were smiling. The first one said, "I bid you peace and joy. Art's face lit up." He ran over to the women and hugged them. "Nyssa, Lysta! Boy, am I glad to see you!" "We are happy to see you as well," said Nyssa. Art did not recognize the last woman. She bowed slightly and said "Welcome to Vada. I think you refer to it as the planet Mars." Will could not believe his eyes. He could not stop starring at the woman who stood before him. She was a beautiful, statuesque woman with a deep dark chestnut completion, short black hair, and deep smokey eyes. She wore tight fitting work clothes with boots and gloves. It was obvious to Will that she was not from the planet Lazon. Everyone noticed the intense eye contact between the two. Matt and Will went over to greet them. "Who's your friend?," asked Will. "I didn't catch her name." Lysta made the introductions. "Will this is Nibila, proud owner of this fine vessel. Nabila, this is Will from planet Earth and these are his partners Art, and Matt." "It is a pleasure to meet you." The two were still staring as they shook hands. Matt got straight to the point. "Why all the cloak and dagger?" Matt could see that the women did not understand his human lingo. "Sorry. Why did you bring us here instead of coming to us?" Nyssa's expression turned serious. "We were sent by the council of Earth's Guardians. The Galactic Alliance has been monitoring events on your home planet and is quite puzzled at the lack of countries willing to take Ruler Rotart up on his bogus offer. They are aware that the humans have no means of discovering his pilot to deceive you but yet your continued efforts to build new ships during his one-year absence have caused the Alliance to call into question weather or not Earth has been receiving outside assistance. In short, Earth is being investigated. It is far too risky for us to come to Earth so, here you are. I will ask you for a progress report later but for now, as you know those who stay behind on Earth are at great risk. Most of the underground shelters, are not sound and will not withstand the impact of the collision with the planet Teldaran or the fires and floods that will surely follow in the aftermath. Due to Rotarts folly, millions maybe billions of humans will die. The inhabitants of this planet are experts in building such subsurface structures. Take a look around I am sure that you will agree. Come aboard and we will tell you what has been going on since our last visit." After several encounters with alien races, Will knew that the key to finding out the origin of an alien being is to get a look at their palm print. During dinner, Will made his move. "Say Nabila, you are not from Lazon are you?" "No" answered Lysta "She is from..." Nabila was quick to cut her off. "I am from a planet far away in another star system. Another galaxy. Twice a year I pick up food from Tagalon and deliver the produce here to Vada." She noticed Will looking at her gloved hands. Nablia smiled at him and said, "Dismiss the thought human." Each encounter with the alien allies was a learning experience for the guys.

The group sat around amonget the large crates and boxes finishing off a hearty meal as Lysta served a fruity yellow beverage that taste a lot like wine. Nyssa gave some background on the host planet, and why they chose to rendezvous there. "The inhabitants of this planet are master builders of subterranean structures," she said. "A few years ago, the galactic menace Rotart attempted to terra-form this planet. The result was massive explosions and a quake that would have registered 14.0 using Earths measurement on the Richter scale." It would seem that from previous debates that Art would have learned by now that Nyssa was hardly ever wrong. Undaunted, Art leaned forward and poked his finger into the air to interrupt Nyssa yet again. "I am sorry Nyssa, but you said 14.0. You see, that's not possible. The Richter scale only goes to 10.0." "Thank you Art for making my point. Had this occurred on Earth most of your structures would have turned into rubble, thousands of humans would have been buried alive if they had occupied the underground shelters in their current state." She paused for effect and looked directly into Arts eyes. "The Vadarians, on the other hand, have suffered no loss of life and only minor structural damage. This is why you were summoned here. To learn and teach your people how to survive in the under life." Lysta and Nyssa spoke like a verbal tag team, each often finishing the others thought or sentence. Lysta cut in again. "There is a price for this knowledge," said Lysta. She paced around the cargo as she spoke. "Earth's Guardians has an ally on the council of Oracles. We have learned that in the not to distant future two major events will occur. One, New earth will become a member of the Galactic Alliance and shortly after, this planet, the one you call Mars will be invaded by the Ortarians. Rotart has deemed this planet as uninhabitable in its present form. He is mindful of the physical changes that his race will undergo if they settle underground here. You see, without the natural sunlight and fresh air the pigmentation is lost and over time your height will decrease. You will see when you meet your host. Do not be alarmed by their appearance."

Nabila was growing impatient. She had left the group and was now yelling from atop one of the crates stored in the back. "Nyssa, could you speed things up a bit! I have a ship to unload!" Will scratched his head. "I'm a bit confused," he said. "What does the Ortarians invasion of Vada have to do with Earth?" "I don't know about Earth," yelled Nabilla from behind a stack of boxes she was caring. "I do know that the Vadaians have been very good to me not to mention that almost twenty percent of my business comes from this planet." "The answer is plain," said Nyssa. "The Vadaians will help to save millions of human lives now in exchange for your word that the humans will vote in favor of the Planetary Alliance's decision to build a defense outpost to protect them from Rotart's invasion in the future." "Now, I am confused." said Matt. "Didn't you just say that Rotart didn't want to live here?" "You heard correctly," said Nyssa. "However, Rotart will not live forever and the Council of Oracles predicts that Rotart's son Taz, will soon rise to power. He will grow tired of seeking a new home for his people and will seek refuge here because it is defenseless. There will be others who will vote to protect Vada but it has been foretold that New Earth will have the deciding vote. It is, as you humans like to say a win, win situation. If you three are in agreement we can began the tour and we will have you back home in a few days." Again, Nabila yelled from the back of the room. "Come on you guys! Say yes. In a couple of years, you will all be heroes here and back on Earth. I mean New Earth. Come on, let's get this show on the road." Art stood up scratching his head. "Are you sure this is going to work?" Nabila jumped from off of one of the crates and stood with her elbow on Lysta's shoulder. "The Thinkers are rarely wrong, and the Oracles. Well, they are never wrong." After holding a private conference, the men agreed to go through with the deal. "We're in," said Matt.

Shortly thereafter, they were introduced to one of the planet's representative refered to as, The Thinker. He communicated telepathically through Nabila who relayed his thoughts to the others. This was by far the oddest encounter the three men have witnessed since it all began six years ago. "Many thousands of years ago, there was a great shift in the climate of the planets surface. As a matter of survival, our ancestors sought refuge down here hundreds of meters below the surface. Our society is not one run by leaders who wave their arms about making speeches filled with false promises. Ribbon cutting and baby kissing is a waste of time. I am one of seven Thinkers on the entire planet." As Nabila spoke the words of the strange looking man Will could not help but wonder how odd it was to hear those words coming out of her mouth. Although they had just met it seemed out of character for someone so loose and laid back. "We are referred to as The Thinkers," she said. "Our sole purpose is to solve the problems faced by our society just as those who came before us and like those who will follow. Please except our gratitude in advance. You will be given total access to all areas of our planet. Feel free to ask any questions, but be warned. Many of our race has never encountered a human before. We are curious to learn more about your people. Especially you Mr. Will. I see that your aide has arrived. Tyi, will proceed with the tour. I must rejoin my counterparts. We have much to ponder on this day. It is a challenging responsibility but it is very rewarding." Nabila introduced the men to Tyi and turned to leave. Will gently grabbed her by the arm. "Hey, not so fast. Where are you going? We need you." Nabila smiled at Will and removed his hand from her arm. "No, you don't." She replied. "Did you forget that the Vadarians are on the ship waiting to help me unload? I only have three days to make the delivery. You will be fine. Just touch his hand." Said Nabila. Will made a funny face at her. "What?" he said. "Just do it, will you." Tyi held out his tiny grey hand and Will slowly reached for it.

When he made contact, he heard a voice in his head say "Hello Will, my name is…" Will jerked his hand away from the little man and quickly ducked behind Nabila. She laughed so hard that she tripped and fell into Will's arms. "Sorry," she said once she was back on solid footing. "That was so funny. It took me years to understand and speak their language, but they also communicate with a simple touch. An arm, or shoulder, any body part will do. Meet me back at the ship when you're done." Matt, Will, and Art decided to take turns holding on to the shoulder of their guide. He told them that his name was Tyi. He led them down a long narrow dimly lit path with high walls covered in a yellow glowing flores-cent substance. When they approached the opening, what they saw totally blew them away. "This is zone 42." said the guide as he slowly waved his hands toward the humongous cavern. "Behold!" "I see it but I don't believe it," said Art.

The men were awe struck by the vastness of the gigantic bustling city that lay before them. It was the size of at least six football fields with ceilings over 30 sto-ries high. There were windows and walkways with railings spiraling upward on either side of each level of the complex. Tyi pointed toward the upper levels. "Dwellings" repeated Matt as he held onto the shoulder of the guide. "This is one of many areas that we call home. All commerce and trade take place here on the bottom level." He then pointed to the trees, foliage, and various other planets that lined the walls and dotted the pathways above. This represents a tiny fraction of our echo system. The lights gave off an amber glow. Art, Matt, and Will marveled at the technology as hundreds of Vadaians went about their normal business. A few stopped to stare at them but most went about their daily routines. Our people have been given word of your arrival. They are both grateful and ashamed. "Why would they be ashamed?," said Will. Tyi grabbed Will's hand and placed it on his shoulder.

"About a hundred years ago, he said. A rouge society of scientists from our planet began abducting humans in an effort to reverse the height loss and size of our appearance. These abductions were strictly forbidden by the Thinkers, but a group of zealots secretly banded together and vowed to continue until a solution was found. They believe that your human DNA holds the key to restoring our physical stature and more." Tyi did not seem comfortable discussing it. He pointed to the large tunnel openings at each end of the complex. The narrow space ran from the base to the ceiling with futuristic looking trains coming and going on the ground below while passenger air shuttles emerged and disappeared into the blackness of the tunnel on the opposite sides. The trains made a slight hissing sound as they glided into the station. Several Vadarians entered quickly and the train silently slid off to its next stop. "This is all very fascinating stuff," said Will "But I have a lot of questions whirling around inside my head. Like, how do you survive down here? Is all of your food shipped in?" "All of your questions will be answered," said Tyi. "Where do I begin? Ah, follow me please."

Tyi lead them down another dark passageway and into an elevator that went down even farther. "This is the floor," he explained. "Un friggin believable," said Matt. Art touched the ground and picked up a fist full of soil. "This can't be real." "I can assure you all that what you see before you is quite real indeed." Will, Matt, and Art were standing on the fringe of a fully-grown forest complete with plants, flowers, shrubs, and grass. "What you see my human friends took more than a thousand years to create. We have a total of nine underground forests on Vada. The water is shipped in as glaciers in specially equipped ships. The mist overhead supplies the necessary water to maintain what you see while the ultra violet lights do the rest. You may recognize many of these plants. Our collectors procured them from many planets including Earth." Art didn't know what to think. He was annoyed, amazed, and a bit angry all at once. "You mean to tell me that you stole all of this from other planets." Tyi remained clam. "Tell me Art, how does one go about stealing something of no value that sits out in the open in great quantities? These have no value to you. Our people were dying and now we are a thriving society. Your trees have given us life. Tell me, has anyone on Earth reported any missing trees in the last century? I think not. Then the matter is closed."

After the first day's tour they could hear the melodic sounds of the woodwinds playing over the PA system as everyone headed back to Nabila's ship. Suddenly, the amber lights began to flicker and Tyi motioned for everyone to stop. A few seconds later, the entire compound was awash in soft soothing purple lights. "This represents our nightfall." he explained. "The ultra violet is used to help our plants grow and it also puts you in a more relaxed state of mind. Peaceful, don't you agree? Tomorrow our master builders will show you how all of this was created so that you can share that knowledge with your people."

When the men returned to the ship dinner was already on the table. Will was certain that he would get a glimpse of the palm of Nabila's hand but it wasn't in the cards. The gloves stayed on. Art decided to use the direct approach. "Say Nabila, do you ever take those gloves off?" "My my," she shook her head. "You humans sure are a curious bunch. Why yes," she responded. "These are my dinner gloves my work gloves are in the back. Would you like to borrow them?" Nabila knew full well what Art was driving at. She was amused by the puzzled look on his face. After dinner Nabila turned to Will and gave him a mischievous grin. She extended her hand. "Come Will. Walk with me. I want to introduce you to a few of my friends." As soon as the two were out of sight Art and Matt practically begged Lysta, and Nyssa to tell them everything they knew about the mysterious Nabila. The women were reluctant at first but after the guys swore never to breathe a word; Lysta began to spill the beans.

"Nabila is from the planet Rayothen, well her ancestors were. Years ago, her species were forever disgraced by the greed that destroyed thier entire planet. Almost a thousand years ago, the Rayothens discovered great wealth right under their feet in the form of precious stones. The deeper they dug the more beautiful and valuable the stones. For centuries, they exported the gems to every known planet in the galaxies and became very, very wealthy. It's been told that some in distant planets used the precious gems to build wonderful homes, and magnificent cities with the most beautiful roads the eye has ever seen. The Rayothens even invented larger machines to dig deeper and faster. This created many large craters some as deep as a mile down and a quarter mile across. Then it happened, the tons and tons of stones removed from the planet over the years caused the planet to shift gradually and the tremors began. However, the inhabitants of Rayos were so overcome with greed they continued to dig until one day the planet began to gradually cave in on it's self. Years later, when the problem could no longer be ignored the rulers finally decided to build a massive ship large enough to house those who had remained on Rayothen. They knew of the peril that was to come so they used their great wealth to construct the vessel in four parts with a hub that when combined created an artificial planet. Shortly after its completion the planet was abandoned and the entire planet of Rayothen imploded with great fury. This reckless, careless, disregard for their own planet is a stigma that still haunts them to this very day. They have been forever shamed. Most planets will allow them to visit but none will allow them to settle down for fear of history repeating itself." Art shook his head. "I don't get it. That was hundreds of years ago." Matt stood up to stretch his legs. He turned to Art and said "The sins of the parents. But, what's up with the gloves?" "What Nabila conceals is the sign of the spiral." Nyssa pointed to her hand to demonstrate. "They have no home. They are called Nomados or Numidian if you prefer. It means wandering tribe. Their once proud race has been tarnished forever." "Such a shame."said Lysta. Just then, the entire city went dark. "What's going on?" Matt asked. "Looks like a power failure." Before anyone could answer white pulsating strobe lights flashed throgh the darken city. "This cannot be good." said Lysta.

In the distance, Nyssa noticed two figures racing toward them. It was Nabila and Will. "Intruders!" Yelled Nabila. "Come on, we have to go now!" They all ran as fast as they could toward the center of the city until they ran into Tyi. Nabila was the only one able to read his thoughts. "Otarians!" She shouted. "If you are discovered all will be ruined. All the spaceports have been shutdown. The soldiers have begun searching zones one thru nine." Nabila continued to act as Tyi's translator. After explaining what she had learned from Tyi, she sent him back into the city to see what other information he could find out. Using the narrow back passageways, Nabila guided the others to the family dwellings on the top level of the town. "From this vantage point you can view the marketplace as well as most of the city", she explained. She took them inside one of the houses and introduced them to the family that lived there. She pulled the two who appeared to be the parents aside. When they came back, Nabila looked a bit more at ease. "These are my friends," she explained. "You will be safe here." The three children two boys and a girl just starred at their new alien houseguest. Nyssa flopped down into the chair and covered her eyes with her hands. "We have failed our mission. Billions of humans may die. How did they find us?" Nabila knelt down beside her. "We are not failures. The battle can and will be won. This," she looked around her, "is a very special place. We will prevail." Will and Matt were standing guard at the windows. The flashing lights had stopped. Will called out "Guys, the purple lights have come back on." "Yea," said Matt. "There is movement in the courtyard but no sign of Rotart's army yet." The women decided that now was the best time to hide the Sprite before the Otarian army discovered it. Nabila headed for the door. "Since I am the only one who can move around freely, I will program the ship to return to an isolated location back on Earth. I will send it through one of the surface vents. It is a small vessel so the soldiers should not notice its departure on the monitor." Before Art could ask his question, Nabila had stepped outside and vanished into the purple haze. Art turned to Will and Matt, "Just how in the world are we supposed to get home?" Will gave him a nervous laugh. "Jumping the gun a bit don't you think?," said Will. "Rotart's goons are all over the place. I don't think that he's going to give up until he finds us and hands us over to the Planetary Alliance on a silver platter." The older male Vadarian grabbed hold of Art's hand. "Do not despair my pale friend. No harm will come to you or your friends. I am the ancestor of the Great Architect. This is a special place. Many places to keep you out of harms way," he said.

The next morning Nabila returned with news. Last night, I was stopped by Taz. "Don't worry. It was after I sent the Sprite on her way. His men searched my ship. After questioning me, he decided to let me go." "Taz!" Repeated a stunned Nyssa. "What in Yeshua's name is he doing here?" Once again Art felt left out. "Who the bloody hell is Taz?" he asked. Nabila gave Nyssa and Lysta an odd look. "Weren't you listening? We told you yesterday. Taz is the son of Rotart. He is twice as bad as his Father is. The good news is that he is not after you people. He is searching for the Thinkers. Taz has discovered the food storage facilities and has threatened to confiscate one bin for each day that the Thinkers stay in hiding. Taz believes that the Thinkers can come up with a solution to the overcrowding on the Otarians home world." "He's probably acting on his own," said Nyssa. "Taz now realizes that Rotarts plan will fail so he is looking for a new home and time is running out." Nabila knew that the Thinkers were not afraid of Taz and his Army but she was concerned that the Vadarians would not have enough food to last the season if Taz begins to pillage their supplies as promised. "The Thinkers will turn themselves in when the time is right," said Nabila. "They are probably discussing it as we speak."

There was a commotion in the village square below. Lysta ran to the window. "Soldiers," she whispered to herself. Nabila walked up behind her to see for herself. "Oh no! Soldiers!" Yelled Nabila. "Hundreds of them." She grabbed Will by the hand and almost pulled his arm out of the socket. "Hurry, everyone. This way." She led them to a small back room where she jumped on a chair to remove a panel in the ceiling. Will watched as she struggled to pull the blue lever down. Nabila, move over. Will climbed onto the chair and yanked the lever until it moved freely. Will heard a hissing sound and watched as the back wall slide open. Once they entered the secret room, the Father Vadarian closed the entrance and replaced the panel in the ceiling. The secret room led to a series of dimly lit narrow corridors. Matt took a quick head count. "Everybody's here, man that was close "he whispered. They could hear voices on the other side of the wall. Taz's men had entered the house. "This way."whispered Nabila as she pointed toward the narrow staircase. "This was the home of the ancient Master Architect. I told you that it was special. When he designed these cities, he decided to add a little something extra to protect his family. This little hideaway and the catacombs under the city did not show up on any of his designs." Matt and Will had to crouch down to keep from hitting their heads on the low ceilings. "Where are we going, asked Matt? My back is killing me." Nabila looked over her shoulder at Matt. "Not much further Matt. I am taking you back to the spaceport where my ship is. They have already searched the ships. It is unlikely that they would return." Another day went by before the Thinkers turned themselves in to Taz's soldiers. Tyi brought the good news and the blueprints for Matt, Art, and Will to take back to Earth. But there was also bad news. As promised Taz emptied three of the food storage bins even though the Thinkers came forward in only two days. The people of Vada would survive but they would have to adjust to the shortage. Nabila had no choice but to offer the stranded men a lift back to Earth. She was happy to do it because it gave her more time to get to know Will.

"Sorry we dragged you into this," said Nyssa. Nabila smiled. "I do not mind the detour now that my cargo has been delivered." Lysta called Nabila over to the ships computer. "Nabila, you said that you programmed the Sprite to land on Earth in an isolated area. Show me where it is so that they can retrieve it upon their return home." Nabila stepped closer to the screen. She seemed proud of the spot she chose to hide the ship. "It is here. I sent it to this large crater in the ground. No one will ever find it there." Everyone was now gathering around the computer screen. They all looked at one another but no one wanted to break the news to Nabila. Finally, Will put his arm around her and smiled. "You sent the Sprite to one of the biggest tourist attractions on the entire planet. This," he pointed to the screen, "is the Grand Canyon." Nabila was baffled. She though for a moment and shook her head. "I do not understand. It's a hole in the ground. You humans are a very strange species indeed. Why spend time and wages to travel hundreds of miles to look at a gigantic hole in the ground?" Everyone burst into laughter.

A few hours later, Nabila maneuvered the freighter into earth's atmosphere. She called Will over and said, "This time you choose." Will chuckled. "Just drop us off somewhere that's isolated." Nabila elbowed him in the ribs. "Not funny," she said. "Okay, okay." Will grabbed his ribs with one hand and pointed to the map with the other. "How about here? We want to attract as less attention as possible." The freighter landed in a wooded area after dark. The guys thanked the ladies and said goodbye. Will and Nabila walked away from the ship and hid behind a large oak tree to have one last private moment. "I will see you again," he promised. They kissed and Will watched as she boarded the ship with Nyssa and Lysta. When the ship disappeared into the clouds the men felt relieved. It was good to be back on American soil and out of danger. The mission was a success. Matt called Eric on his cell phone. It took two days before Eric's people were able to locate Will, Art, and Matt. On the night of the landing they checked into a small county style bed and breakfast and enjoyed the hospitality of the friendly locals in a sleepy little town called Kiptopeke somewhere on the Eastern shore in Virginia.

CHAPTER 17

▼

NEPTUNE'S EYE
REDUX

A blanket of new fallen snow covered the landscape on the road to the airport. As Art maneuvered his car through the holiday traffic, he thought how fitting it was to have a white Christmas on the last Christmas on Earth. During the last two years, Art shuttled back and forth between Washington and London. The P.M was true to his word. Art is now Sir Arthur. Julie's flight was on time for a change. "Happy Christmas, sweetheart." They embraced and exchanged gifts in the airport terminal. "Go on luv, open it," said Julie with a smile. Art ripped the red sparkling wrapping paper off and opened the box. It was a book. "Hey, hon. I think you are going to have to return this. Look all the pages are blank," said Art with a straight face. Julie realized that Art was putting her on. "Oh Artie, stop pulling my leg! It's a journal, you know, to write your memoirs." Art examined the large brown leather book with the gold tip pages. "I love it," he said, "and I love you. Now open yours." Julie looked down at the blue box but resisted the urge to open it. Tiffany's she though to herself. "Oh Artie, I think I'll wait until we get home. Is there any chance of getting out of this dinner party?" She asked. "Not if you want to stay on Eric's good side." Art replied. "Julie shrugged her shoulders and turned to look out the car window. It's so beautiful. Just like a Norman Rockwell painting."

Julie and Art were the last to arrive at the White House. President Thompson made the introductions. In addition to Will, Sara, and Matt there were Eric, his parents, his wife and 2 sons. The servers brought in enough food to feed a small army. Halfway through dinner one of the President's aides entered the room. "Mr. President, I am really, sorry to interrupt but I think you need to see this." There was a remote on the table a few feet away. It operated the painting on the wall and the TV concealed behind it. The painting rose slowly to reveal the odd situation that was unfolding. That caused everyone to stop eating and congregate around the large screen. "I know that place." Matt pointed. "That statue, it's Christ the Redeemer in Brazil."

The camera operator pulled pack to reveal a UFO hovering just over the top of it. Eric motioned to the aide, "Give us some volume." he ordered. The announcer spoke in Spanish. The best that they could make out was that the ship appeared an hour ago and a large crowd was gathering at the base of The Redeemer. Sara turned to Will, in a voice barely above a whisper she said, "it's Rotart, he's come back." "No," said Eric. "Ship's too small and besides, why would he show up in Brazil? Whoever this is they are sending us a message." "I agree." said Art. "Christ the Redeemer on Christmas Day is a little more than just coincidence." As the dinner guest speculated among themselves. Matt's cell phone was vibrating in his pocket no one noticed him walk to the corner of the room to take the call. "Hello, who is this?" "Hello Matt, you don't know me but for the purpose of this conversation, I am the guy flying the ship you are probably watching on T.V. Before you dismiss this as a prank and hang up, I want you to watch the screen. In exactly fifteen seconds the ship you are watching will assend exactly fifty meters." Seconds later the ship rose just as the voice on the phone predicted. "Okay," said Matt "You have my attention. What do you want? How did you get this number?" The voice on the other end of the phone didn't sound like the other aliens Matt had encountered. He sounded more human. "Have you ever watched the movie Hackers Matt? Never mind, how I got your number is not important. I want to meet with you and your friends Art and Will, but I want assurances from President Thompson that we will not be taken into custody or attacked." Just then the President called out to Matt from across the room. "Matt, we could use your help over here. We need to find out who these jokers are." Matt stunned everyone in the room with his next remark. "I know who they are. Well, actually I know how to reach them." Matt handed Eric the phone. "It's for you."

Eric knew that Matt would never joke at a time like this. The alien on the phone was male. "Mr. President, I know you to be a man of your word, a man of honor." Thompson gave the alien his word and the alien gave Eric the time and coordinates of the mysterious pow-wow. The National Security advisor and Homeland Security was called in as well as the Coast Guard. Eric filled everyone in. "Ladies and gentlemen, in spite of my assurances it seems that our alien friends still do not trust us. We don't know if these are the good guys or the bad guys. There is always the possibility that we could have a new player. A third alien race." General Wayborn entered the room and handed the President a map. "Well sir, the General pointed to the map. At least they have a sense of humor. We checked the longitude and latitude three times. These are the coordinates that that they gave us." President Thompson placed the map in the middle of the table so that the others could see. There was a red x marked directly in the center of the Bermuda triangle. Eric looked at Matt, Art, and Will. "Are you sure that you boys are up for this?" Art pulled the map toward him for a closer look. "Mr. President. I don't' think we have a choice. They know who we are. God only knows what else they know." Matt looked at Sara as he nodded in agreement with Art. He knew that she did not want him to go but she also knew that the stakes were high and that Matt needed to support the team. Matt turned to Eric. "Mr. President we have less than a year to go. If this is another of Rotart's tricks, we need to know about it." Will was already heading for the door. "Come on guys." Will waved them on without looking back. We are wasting time. "Let's do it."

The sea was cold and dark when the Coast Guard cutter dropped the three men off on to a smaller craft and moved off about a quarter mile. It did not take long for the aliens to show. It was the same ship from Brazil. Once the men were aboard the ship submerged deep into the frigid ocean waters. Matt could not help but notice how small this ship was in comparison to the others. In the center of the ship was a round table made of frosted glass. Tinted amber light came from the base of the table as well as from overhead. Matt could only see two aliens aboard. The female did most of the talking. "I am Zonola and this is Harry." Zonola could read the puzzled looks on their faces. "I will explain later. Please, have a seat." Harry came over with a tray. "Would anyone care for a beverage?" He asked. "We have Pepsi, Ginger ale, Dr. Pepper and Penta Water." Will leaned over to whisper in Art's ear. "This is just too weird man. A jeans wearing Pepsi drinking alien named Harry. I think I ate too much turkey. The tryptophan must be kicking in." Matt got right down to business. "No, thank you. Show me your hands," he demanded.

Harry returned the drinks to the galley and they both laid their hands on the table palms up. "Otarians," he whispered. "What do you want? Did Rotart send you?" Zonola looked at Harry before answering Matt. "Rotart is dead." She said in a clam voice. "Dead." said Will. "How?" "He was assassinated at the hands of his own son. Rotart was about to give a speech in front of thousands of Otarians. Right before he was to begin, his son Taz and his henchmen forced fed him a triple dose of clear and shoved him onto the balcony before the chanting crowd. A few seconds later, he simply exploded. I hear they had to use a mop and bucket to collect his remains. Yes, it is a fact that we share the same heritage of being Otarians but the similarities end there. You see we are more human than you think. The only thing that separates you from us is a half a dozen internal organs. Oprah, Harry Potter, J Lo, "Imus in the Morning" and "Hardball with Chris Matthews"are a part of our culture just as it is yours. Nine eleven was as real for us as it was for humans around the world. We have asked you here because we seek asylum. We are prepared to earn it as well as your trust. There are a total of seventeen of us." Matt held up his hand "Stop!" he said. "There is nothing in our laws that will allow us to give you sanctuary even if the President did agree. For crying out loud, you guys are from another planet. A planet hell bent on destroying us." Harry showed Matt the palm of his hand. "Do not be fooled by the mark of the Otarian. Earth is the only home that we have ever known. We were all born and raised here. Our home is beneath the sea in Neptune's Eye.

On the night that you three made first contact with the Lazon's, Zonola and I were on patrol. That night we decided not to report the meeting to our supervisors because we knew that it would doom your entire race. The Eye of Neptune was once occupied by two hundred of us but seventeen of us volunteered to stay behind. You are aboard a scout ship. It is not capable of traveling in deep space. In four days time, our orders are to rendezvous with The Tyborg and return to Otar."

Art, Will, and Matt didn't know what to make of their story. Will as usual was still not convinced. "Okay let's say we believe you. Why show yourselves now?" Zonola pointed to the map on the wall. "We don't want to be stowaways or spend the rest of our lives in hiding. But there is a bigger reason. You see Will, we are not asking for charity. We have information that could save millions of lives, human lives." She nodded to Harry. Harry sat at the controls and they could feel the ship leave the water as it headed skyward. "Please, do not be alarmed. After Rotart's plans failed, he had one more ace up his sleeve. In a few minutes, we will arrive at the Astral Corridor. You call them portals. All of your ships are programmed to seek out these Corridors in order to reach the Intergalactic Flash Lanes. These streams as we call them propel ships through space at amazing speeds. Each of your ships are programmed to proceed to a specific gate or portal marked by the pyramids located exactly sixty-two and one half miles above the Earth. Ah, we are here. Gentlemen come to the window. There." Zonola pointed. There was a massive blue and white ball of swirling gases. "This is one of the portals." Zonola explained. Art was shaken by what he saw. "Hey! There are two ships out there." Harry rejoined the group. "Lazorian War ship to be exact," said Harry. Will and Matt were also uneasy. Will turned to Harry. "Glad you cleared that up for us. Why are they there?" "They are Centurians" replied Zonola in a serious tone. "They are here to protect the gate until all of your ships have passed through next year." Again, she motioned to Harry. "Number two, please. The gate you guys just saw was at the Pyramid of the Sun in Mexico, this is also in Mexico. It's the one you refer to as Chichen Itza."

The three went back to the window expecting to see the blue and white swirl and the Centaurian ships. To there surprise there was only darkness. Art squinted his eyes thinking he had missed it the first time. Harry chuckled; "Don't waste your time Art. It ain't there." All eyes turned to Harry. "There's a simple explanation," said Harry. "Rotart blew it up along with the ones in Peru, Spain, Germany and a couple of others. He would have destroyed them all if it were not for The Planetary Alliance. They are the ones you can thank for sending the centuries to protect the ones that are left. Many years ago, our ancestors discovered the gateways and corridors. It took years to map out just this one solar system. It was decided that the pyramids were the best way to permanently mark the entrances so a few of our people privately offered the technology as burial shrines to the kings and rulers of that era in hopes that something so sacred would stand the test of time." Zonola smiled at Harry. Thank you Harry. "You can take us back home now. What do you mean home." Matt was beside himself. "We have thousands of ships. Are you telling me that they are all supposed to travel through that one portal!" Will grabbed Matt and pulled him back into the chair. Will was staring at Zonola but talking to Matt. "Don't you get it? It's time for lets make a deal. If you show me yours, I will show you mine. If we take them in they will show us where all of the functioning Portal Gates are and as a bonus, I guess they will show us how to reprogram the ships computers to lock on to the new entrances. How am I doing Zonola? Lady you may not be Rotart but you sure as hell have learned a few of his moves."

Zonola tried to reason with Will. "What would you do if you were in my place? We are taking all of the risk. What if there are spy's about? Rotart may be gone but his son is still alive and kicking. Would you have us return to Otar, another doomed planet? We will earn our keep. Tell President Thompson we will tell what we know. Here is my cell phone number. One last thing Mr. Will.

Harry was not his given name, he chose it to feel more American. All we ask is that you do not judge us before getting to know us. If we do not hear from you in two days, we will have no choice than to follow our orders and leave Earth." They were about to leave but Will could not resist one more question. "By the way, what are the rest of your orders?" Zonola seemed only too happy to respond. "Our orders are to blow up Neptune's Eye and all the technology with it. Good night, gentlemen. If I hurry, I can still catch the opening monologue on Leno."

President Thompson quickly realized that he had no choice but to comply with the request of the aliens. Area 54 was a secret government installation in the hills of Vermont not far from Smugglers Notch. Twenty stories underground was a state of the art lab, for conducting highly classified science experiments and a weapons lab. Two stories below the lab were living accommodations that would put any four star hotel to shame. The director of the facility gave Harry, Zonola and the fifteen other men, women and children the tour. "Welcome to your new home. This is where you will live for the next year." After the tour, Zonola and Harry were taken to a meeting room upstairs where the top military brass questioned them about their base. By the time Eric and the guys arrived a large van with blacked out windows was pulling up to the entrance to carry everyone to the scout ship. In no time at all, the ship was plunging into the darkness as it headed to the bottom of the ocean 7 miles below. Will's eyes were locked onto the window next to his seat. Not speaking to anyone in particular he said. "Man, this is not what I signed on for. It's broad daylight but it looks like the middle of the night." The ship started to slow down. Will could make out to the outline of the base from the ships light reflecting off its blue outer hull. It was massive and that was not counting what was beneath the ocean's surface. General Wayborn could not believe his eyes. "Well I'll be damned," he said. "I thought this was a bunch of horse manure. All these years we were looking the wrong way. Well I guess I have seen it all."

Two large doors slowly began to open and Harry piloted the small ship inside. Once the ship came to a stop Zonola showed the group around. "This technology may seem advanced by your standards but because of the problems on Otar, we can't even get spare parts. Everything you see here is at least 12 years old." The General and his men were like kids in a candy store. Everyone had questions. The White House even sent along a photographer. President Thompson called for everyone's attention. "Ladies and gentlemen, let's not lose our focus. Find out what will be useful to us in the future." General Wayborn shook his head. "Mr. President most of this equipment is stuff that we have never seen before and we haven't covered half of the base yet. Were gonna need at least a week to figure out what the hell we got there sir." Eric turned to Zonola she smiled at the General. She and her people had been granted asylum by the President himself. Now she was not only willing but also eager to prove her loyalty. "I am at your disposal. Take all the time you need." Zonola and Harry had delivered as promised.

Will felt bad about coming down so hard on her the other day. Later that evening Zonola received a package. It was the complete anthology of Motown on CD. The note inside the package was simple and to the point. It read, "sorry, I misjudged you. Will." Not all the news was good. Early the next morning Harry flew the team to all of the Portal Entrances then dropped them off at the White House where the President anxiously awaited their report. "Three! Only three are you certain?" President Thompson did not take the news very well. "Yes," said Matt "we, used the pyramid chart from the crop circles and Harry even took us to a few that weren't on the list. Out of the 19 Astral Corridors, only three remains in tact. The great Pyramid at Giza, the Pyramid of the Sun in Mexico, and the White Pyramid in China. These are the only routes left that can take us to the Flash Lanes." Will was quick to back up Matt's report. "I am afraid he's right Eric. Rotart really did a number on us after all. Even in death, he's still putting the screws to us." Art did not want the men to feel as though they had been defeated. He decided to take a positive approach to the problem. "Mr. President, it may not be as bad as it looks." I am listening said Eric. "Well, according to Harry each ship is programmed to gravitate towards any portal within a thirty-mile radius sort of like a tractor beam you see on those science fiction movies. The Lazons knew that our pilots have no experience so they also equipped each ship with something called a buffer." said Art. "Well sir, it's actually a safety mechanism that prevents the ships from crashing into one another. When the on board clocks reach zero we start sending the ships through. If the Council of Oracles are right we can get all of the ships through in time."

Matt was furiously tapping numbers into a calculator while Art talked to Eric. Eric's expression turned from one of deep despair to hope. "Art I think you may be on to something. It's going to be close but if we establish a country by country order…" Matt handed Eric a diagram that he had sketched out with three circles and the globe representing Earth beneath it. "Yes," said the President after studying Matt's drawings. "If we can get everyone to agree, we may still be able to pull this off. Gentlemen, I believe the good Lord is looking out for us." Without Zonola and Harry this whole thing would have ended in disaster. Will gave Matt a high five. "Amen brother."

CHAPTER 18

▼

THE CALM BEFORE
THE STORM

Sara watched as the painters applied the finishing touches to the new Space Force one logo on the side of the ship that sat on the White House lawn. Ships worldwide were given a name and an identification number. Every state held a contest to select the names of the ships in their area. Sara and Matt had completed the projects assigned to them by Eric. They decided to enjoy the beautiful spring day by having a cookout under the Cherry Blossom trees near the lake. The Chef prepared a basket with Sara's favorite foods and wine. As they sat on the blanket watching the sailboats drift by Matt was fully aware that this may be the last time they would be able to enjoy this place before leaving Earth forever. Sara began to weep. "I am sorry Matt but I can't do this." Matt rushed over to comfort her. "Do what babe? What's going on?" Sara tried to regain her composure. "I just spent the better part of the three years working with the underground people, the so-called bottom dwellers. I didn't just teach them how to grow food underground. I have gotten to know them. I have eaten at their tables. I know most of their kids, went to their Birthday parties, weddings, and funerals. How am I supposed to sit here sipping wine and eating brie knowing full well that in less than a year, all of this will be gone and all of them will probably be dead or dying?" Sara began to cry again. Matt handed her a napkin. "I don't know the answer babe. The reality is they have chosen to stay. With a little help from the good Lord and the Aliens on Vada who knows they might make it. You know that better than I do. Their religious belief won't allow them to leave and we have to respect that." "I tried Matt I really did but, I don't' know. It took years for me to get over losing our baby and now this. I pray every night that they change their minds."

Matt took Sara home and they ran into Eric in the lobby. "Well if it isn't two of my favorite people beautiful day, isn't it?" Sara looked at Eric and continued on to her room. "It is something I said? You guys should be doing cartwheels. In seven months, we will be on our way. A minor miracle don't ya think?" Matt filled Eric in on the details of the picnic and Sara's depression. "Listen Matt, all of our ships are ready to go, the last of the ships that we promised to the U.N. be ready next month. Zonola, Harry and their clan are happily tucked away at Area 54, and O yea, Rotart's dead. I think we are fortunate. Come on Matt only ninety-two percent of our citizens are coming to the new planet. And Taz is still out there somewhere. I understand Sara's feelings but we are not miracle workers. She'll get over it in time. What are we supposed to do kidnap them? Force them on the ships at gunpoint? If she wants to feel sorry for someone tell her to feel sorry for those poor bastards in France or Germany or Russia. There the one's getting screwed. Hey, I'm late for a meeting. I will talk to Sara if you think it would do any good." "I don't think so Eric, but thanks any way."

As the weeks went by Matt's state of mind began to change. He went through sudden periods of frustration for no apparent reason except one, T'zar. Matt had gone down this road before but this time he was more prepared. Something stressful was going on with T'zar and it was affecting Matt's behavior. He didn't want to burden Sara or Will and Art was spending the final summer with Julie in England. The world seemed off kilter. Sara and Matt spent most of the summer indoors alone. They knew that things would become hectic again beginning July 5th when the ship's crews started to move aboard the ships in preparation for the long journey. They sat and sipped soft drinks while watching the evening news. "What a crazy world." said Matt. "Everyone's either partying or rioting. I guess it depends on what country you live in." "Yeah," agreed Sara, "and it's only going to get worse. The forth of July is not until tomorrow and people have been celebrating for two or three days already. Zack and his people are still transporting supplies underground. I guess they won't be celebrating until all of this is over shh, babe turn it up."

(T.V. Reporter) "Have been forced to beef up security along the U.S border after as many as two hundred foreigners stormed the California Mexico border late last night. "Wow, Matt, they are getting desperate. Mexico has enough ships, where do you think they are coming from? I don't know but I spoke to Eric the other day. He's seriously considering allowing seniors to start boarding the ship in early September after the doctors, and cooks, security, and other essential personnel have moved in. Will's home packing right now, he's moving to Space Force One tomorrow. His quarters will be next to ours." "Matt, Sara, spoke softly, this could get very ugly by the winter. I mean, what if those people who don't have a way off the planet what happens if they make it over here? Are we going to be safe?" Matt pulled Sara close to him. He put his arm around her and kissed her on the cheek. "Of course, we will. Eric has already ordered fences built around the ships in the areas that might be a problem and twenty-four hour security from the military." Sara turned back to the television. The images of cars and buildings in flames didn't help to calm her fears. *Desperate men make desperate moves*, she thought to herself.

A week later Will invited Eric, Sara and Matt to check out his new digs on the ship. Sara and Matt brought a bottle of wine. Will was happy to see them. "Hey, glad you guys could make it. Where's Eric?" Sara handed Will the wine. "Mr. President could not make it." said Sara. "That's cool." said Will. "I'm glad you guys could come. Well," Will spread his arms out to his sides and looked around. "It's small but for the next year or two its home. Unless the aliens have the technology to build instant cities we're all going be living here for a while. Excuse the mess on the desk. You know my family is going to be scattered to the four winds. We decided to set up a website in order to keep in touch and keep tabs on what ships we are going to be on. I was just scanning some pictures onto the site when you showed up." Sara reached for Will's family album. "Will, do you mind? Not at all," he said, "go ahead." Sara looked about halfway through the book of photo's, when she suddenly froze. You could have knocked her over with a feather.

When she was able to get her mind to work along with her mouth, again she called out to Will who was showing Matt around his new living space. "Will! How long have you known Zack?" Will shouted back from across the room. "All of my life, Zachary and I are first cousins; we grew up together in Philly." Sara was floored. For years, she worked underground helping Zack and the under grounders at Sanctuary and the other sites construct the gardens and never made the connection between the two. Sara went from shock to anger. "How in the hell can you just leave him here to die? Don't you care about what happens to him?" Matt had given Will the heads up months ago. That's why he never told her that they were related. "Sara, calm down. I love my cousin like a brother. He's always been a very spiritual guy. We just have different options on the rapture. He believes that the Second Coming will only take place on Earth, this

Earth. I believe that since God made both Earth's that the Lord won't have a problem finding us." "Oh, don't give me that." she snapped back. "What chance do they have of living that long?" Matt helped himself to a glass of wine. He had his own problem to deal with or rather T'zar's problem. Will made another attempt to ease her mind. "Okay Sara, at first I was concerned about his safety. You see Zack's compounds face west and it's built way above sea level." "Yes, go on, Will." "Okay, the Tsunami is coming from the east and it won't reach anywhere near the Adirondacks. The complex is deep underground high in the mountains. That gives them protection from the rain of fire. He didn't pick this place by throwing darts. He's always been a pretty smart guy. Bu there was still one big problem." Matt raised his hand. "Let me guess." Without waiting for a response from Will, Matt blurted out the answer. "Food! If they survive, they may not be able to grow their own food if there is no sun." "Correct." said Will. "However, you changed all of that when you volunteered to help." Sara was starting to put the pieces together. "Will I never..... Eric asked me......She thought for a moment then raised the book over her head and pretended to hit Will with it. you rat! You set me up. You went to Eric after Walker died because you knew Walker would never agree to help them but Eric would. You........why didn't you say? So, they are NOT going to die?" "Not for a very long time." said Will. "Zack had a stress test done on the hulls of the ships before they were placed underground. Just to be sure, he had each one reinforced after we came back from Vada. It's fine for him and his people. I will miss him, but I can't live like that. I am an outdoors kind of guy. In all truthfulness, there are hundreds of underground compounds, some at sea level and barely covered. I can't say how things will turnout for them. We have passed on all of the data from the Thinkers and the others on Vada and that all that we can do. I'm just glad that I can finally thank you for saving my cousin." Will gave Sara a big long hug. "Come on let's eat."

Everyday around four when the sun starts to dip down behind the oak trees Ozzie, Lenny, Tony and Andy meet in New York's Central Park to play cards. Sometimes they play chess or backgammon. Lenny always brings his little black radio. Today it was chess. "We interrupt his broadcast to bring you this live address from the President of the United States." All the men seated around the table were in their seventies. Their hearing is not what it used to be so they leaned inward towards the radio to hear the news. A small crowd gathered around to listen to what the President had to say. "My fellow American's I am speaking to you from the tranquility of the beautiful White House lawn. Unfortunately, things are not as clam in a few countries abroad. Because of the civil unrest in certain regions of the world, I have decided to accelerate the timetable given to me by my Earth 2 advisory team. In order for this evacuation process to operate smoothly and orderly we have already begun boarding all essential personnel such as doctors, ship security, captains, cooks, technicians, and others that are necessary to assure that each vessel will function properly and day to day operations run smoothly. That was the Green Phase or Phase 1. Anyone holding a blue card, this is for seniors, families with expectant mothers, those with medical conditions and their care givers are in Phase 2. Phase 2 will begin boarding on September 7, the day after Labor Day. Phase 3 is anyone holding an orange card. Families with children under eighteen years of age your new move in date is October 1. The final group will consist of everyone not mentioned so far. You should be holding yellow cards. Your move in date will be November 27. If you have any questions just call the number on the card. This updated information is posted on the government website and your local post office." The President's remarks went on for about ten minutes. When it was over Lenny turned down the radio. "Well fellows start packing. You heard the man we move in next week." Ozzie reached for the Queen. "It's about time. I have been packed for a month."

An hour after the announcement in another park miles away in Washington Will stood on the edge of a secluded pond feeding the swans. A black SUV with darkened windows pulled up. The man in the car walked over. Will continued to feed the swans pretending not to notice the man standing next to him. The man looked around at the trees when he spoke to Will. "There was a time when only the walls had ears," said the man. Will looked up at the trees. "Yep, now the ears are everywhere." He reached into his pocket and handed Will a note. The man waited until Will read the message and gave the paper back before continuing. "Think you'll have any problems with that?" Will shook his head no. "Everything's crystal." "Will, you are the only one that I can really trust. Your plane ticket is waiting for you at the ticket counter. You will be picked up when you land. Bring the last box to me." For the first time he looked at Will. "I was never here. We never had this conversation." The man knelt down and placed the note on a flat grey, rock set it on fire and watched it turn into ashes. "I am counting on you to keep this between us Will." Will shook his hand. "Don't worry Mr. President. I won't tell a soul." The President climbed back into the vehicle while Will continued to feed the birds. The black SUV made its way up the winding road through the park and out of sight.

Adjusting to life aboard the ship was an easy transition for Andy and his card-playing friends. The summer sun and heat were no long a problem for Andy and the other seniors. Everyday the four men met in one of the large air-conditioned community centers aboard their new home. Ships around the country were given names like The Georgia Peach, Philadelphia Freedom, and The Seattle Star. Andy's ship was appropriately named the Big Apple. All of the shipboard televisions were located in the community centers. This presented a problem for card players who had to compete with new arrivals mostly women who came to the community room everyday like clockwork. Astrology was now en vogue. Astrologers and astronomers had become the new celebrities replacing singers and movie stars since no new movies were being produced.. Books, posters, websites, and television shows were featuring the now famous astrologers. Up to two hundred women would meet to hear the latest going-ons. Andy and the boys had to take their pinochle games elsewhere. Today was different. It was Thanksgiving. Every community center was converted to a dinning hall so that everyone could enjoy Thanksgiving Dinner together.

Lenny, Tony, Ozzie and Andy invited their new friends Jose and Ralph to sit at their table. Ozzie waved his fork at one of the six television screens on the walls. "What's going on?" He asked. Soon everyone's attention was on the television. The volume was turned up and people were shocked by what they saw and heard. The announcer was in mid sentence. "Live shot of any angry mob storming the ship that is believed to be reserved for Russian authorities," said the reporter. "We are told that the President may also be aboard and they are dragging the occupants from the ship. Security has been over-run. It looks from our vantage point to be at least six hundred people in this angry mob. Earlier today, we spoke to one of the leaders of this group. Here is what he had to say." "Our leaders have failed us. They have decided to leave us here to die a horrible death while they fly away to a carefree new life. Why should we suffer and die for their mistakes? We vow to take every ship with government representatives and replace them with our citizens by force if necessary. These ships belong to us. Our people are frightened and desperate. The world has turned its back on us."

Andy looked around the room. Everyone had stopped eating some were crying others were fighting back the tears. Something had to be done. Without a word, Andy left the room. The community center walls were made mostly of glass so everyone could see Andy as he made his way down the corridor. His friends called after him. "Hey where are you going?" Andy did not answer but continued to move slowly towards his room near the end of the hall. By the time his friends caught up with him, he was standing in his room holding a piece of stone. Jose turned to Lenny, "What's that? A rock?" "No," said Lenny. Before he retired Andy was a reporter, a damm good one. He was in Berlin when the wall fell. That's his prize possession. Chipped it out himself. After studying the rock, Andy pushed through the crowds and walked off the ship. He stopped about thirty feet away from the ship and laid the stone on the ground. When he turned to face the ship hundreds of the ship's passengers were watching him from the windows above. Andy's friends were waiting at the door. The Marines that were posted at the entrance to the ship were amused. "What's up with grandpa?" Said one. Ozzie turned to him and said. "If you don't understand then there's no point in my trying to explain it to you." Lenny, Ozzie, Jose, Tony and Ralph went back to their rooms each following suit by laying a personal item on the ground creating a small pile where Andy's Berlin Wall Rock layed. It didn't take long for the people crowded around the windows to understand what was going on. Word spread quickly around the ship and before nightfall, the pile had grown to over eight feet high. Camera crews with their bright lights began showing up. A reporter stood in front of the pile as more items were added.

"This is a rare site indeed," said the reporter into the camera. "Just the other day members of Congress were pushing for an increase in the amount of weight one could carry aboard ship. Many say this move was due to pressure put on them from wealthy contributors, and here we see the exact opposite: Ordinary people sacrificing just one item in order to save a life. There must be at least six hundred pounds of stuff here so far. That's a family of four that can now ride in place of all these discarded belongings." The reporter reached his hand to his earpiece. "Yes, I am being told that this movement has now caught onto other ships around the country. This reporter has no doubt that the generosity and compassion shown here in the United States will spread throughout the entire world." Eric watched the TV with a few of his aides as the drama unfolded and reports from around the globe started to come in. Eric turned to one of his aides, "We have work to do. Time is of the essence,"he said. "Earl, find out how many people we can take in with the new weight configurations that we have. Andrea, we need to help preserve these people's heritage. I want you to compile a list of historians from each country involved, also language experts, religious teachers, and the like. No fat cats or politicos. Mrs. Robinson, find out exactly how many countries are leaving people. Once we find out how much room we have, we can divide the space up evenly per country. Oh, somebody get Zachary on the phone. I am sure his people could use a lot of that stuff being discarded. Tell security to open the gates and send in a couple of trucks. No, wait. Tell Zack to come tomorrow. Let's make sure that everybody out there gets the message before we start carting everything away." Later that night Andy found himself back in the ships community room. A few hundred of his new friends gave him a party. No astrologers were invited.

CHAPTER 19

▼

EXODUS

The countdown clock atop the corner drug store read 48:00. At that very moment, as if by magic, the main engines on every single ship worldwide suddenly came to life. Sara and Matt could hear the ships engines humming from their bedroom. It was first light but they still noticed that for the first time every light on the ship inside and out was illuminated. "Wow Matt, look it's so beautiful." "Well hon, I guess this is it. Yep," said Matt. "If everything goes according to plan, the first ships should be taking off from St. Andrews in Scotland about six hours from now. We should be on our way by tomorrow afternoon. I sure hope Art and Julie are back from England by then. They are taking a huge risk coming back so late. There are only a few planes still flying." "Well Matt, I don't think they had much choice. It's not as if he got to choose when his grandmother would die." Maybe it was the dim lighting or maybe they were pre-occupied but, neither; Matt or Sara noticed the thin layer of dirt that covered the window ledge overnight.

Art and Julie were a bit more observant, as he and Julie drove to the airport Art posed the question to Julie. "Where do you suppose all this dust is coming from?" "I don't know, Artie; maybe we are going to have a storm." "In December?" He asked. "Well, no matter we will be at the airport soon. Keep your fingers crossed that the last flights haven't been cancelled." Julie went back to reading the paper. She didn't seem to mind that the paper was three days old. All the local newspapers had shut their doors to prepare for the mass departure. The headline across the top of the front page read 'final edition' in big black letters. "Artie, listen to this: It says here that people are gathering in large numbers at holy shrines across the globe. The Wailing Wall, Mecca, Bethlehem, Christ the Redeemer even Stonehenge. How about that?" Art glanced at the paper then focused on the signs leading to where he would drop off the rental. "Bloody fools if you ask me," he said. "Don't they read the papers or watch the Telly? If they don't find shelter by tomorrow they can kiss their butts goodbye."

After checking in Art called Will on his cell. "Well, mate we made it to the airport early but our flights had been delayed. This place looks like a bloody ghost town. The agent at the ticket counter assured me that the flight would be departing in about four and a half hours. It appears that the pilot is American and needs to get back as well." "Okay, buddy call me when you and Julie land I will pick you guys up. See ya." Will returned to the park and stood near where he met with Eric awhile back. He carried a jelly jar from the trunk of his car and paused to look around. He didn't seem to be at all concerned with the chaos that could erupt in the city not far away. Will reached down and filled the jar with dirt. After screwing the top on Will took one last look around as he thought to himself. *I am really going to miss this place.* "What the…" Will began staring into the pond. He squinted to get a better look. Tiny objects were hitting the surface but it wasn't raining. He held out his hand. After a few seconds, he could feel small almost microscopic grains of dirt in his palm. "Something's wrong. I better get back."

Sara and Matt were moving the last of their belonging to the ship when Will caught up with them in the hall. "Matt, Sara, have either of you seen Eric?" Matt could see that something was wrong. "No Will, not since last night. Why? What's up?" "It's starting," explained Will. "Haven't you looked outside?" "Well, yeah, it's cloudy out but so what?" Will became more anxious. "Something is falling from the sky and it ain't pennies from heaven. It feels like sand or dirt. I am not sure what it is. We need to find the President. I've looked everywhere for him." "Come on," said Matt. "Let's drop these boxes off first. Mrs. Robinson once told me that Eric goes to the Truman balcony when he wants to be alone. That's probably where we will find him."

Will took the boxes from Sara and carried them over to the ship. When they reached the lawn, they could see the President staring down at the dirt covered lawn. Matt and Sara could feel the fine dust particles as they gently pelted their faces when they looked up. Will held out his hand. "It's getting stronger, worse than before." The trio joined Eric on the balcony. "Thanks for the update guys, but I got the word about half an hour ago." Eric seemed calm as he spoke about yet another obstacle that had to be overcome. "I've been told that about twenty percent of our people are not on board yet. I just authorized FEMA to put out an emergency announcement telling everyone to go to the ships. Most of the television stations are shut down but two or three radio stations plus short wave is still operating. We were supposed to have another day. The meteorologist told me that the intensity has been increasing hourly since about four this morning. Has anyone heard from Art?" "I have," said Will. "His flight has been delayed but if this stuff starts coming down much harder I don't think the planes are going to fly. We have calculated that it takes 27 hours to get all of the ships through the three gates. It looks like we don't have as much time as we thought. What are we going to do?" President Thompson gazed up at the gray skies. "I spoke to Harry and Zonola this morning. The ships are built to take a hit from meteor showers and such but they are concerned that a steady pounding could cripple them. Our only option is to fly above the storm and wait our turn to enter the gate." "Hold on a minute Eric." Matt didn't like Eric's plan and he wasted no time in letting him know how he felt. "What about Art and Julie? You do remember Art don't you? The guy who cracked the code? Are you just going to leave him stranded?" "I'm sorry Matt. Art will never know how grateful I am for what he has done. For what all of you have done, but I cannot jeopardize the lives of fifty thousand people including you three to save two people. I am sorry." And with that Eric walked away. Deep down Matt knew that Eric had made the right decision, but over the years, Art had become like a brother to him and Will.

As the day progressed people had begun to notice the nut-brown substance as it covered the streets and cars. Their pace began to quicken as they wrapped up last minute chores and said their goodbyes while heading to their designated ships. Will sat by the window watching the tiny grains of dirt that had completely covered the White House lawn when he heard someone knocking. It was Eric. "Hi Will, I am afraid I have some more bad news for you: Effective immediately all aircraft are being grounded by the order of the FAA. There have been a few reports of planes falling out of the sky. Probably due to the dust and dirt being sucked into the plane's engines. Since most of the reporters and camera crews are abroad the ship there is no on one to confirm or investigate the reports and no search and rescues either." Eric handed Will the memo. "Damn! That means that Art and Julie are stranded unless..." Will's voice trailed off. It had occurred to him that they might have been passengers on one of the downed flights. Eric read his mind. "No, Will. Art's flight was cancelled. There is still hope. All the cell phones from the U.S to England are useless." Eric eased Will's mind. "I know I tried to contact him before I came down to see you. So, I contacted the FAA no flights have left Heathrow all day. Just pray that they hitch a ride on one of the ships over there." "One more bit of happy news. The storm is getting worse." Eric said grimly. "You want me to break it to Matt?" Will asked. "I was kinda hoping you would offer to." Eric continued. "Thanks. You two are closer. I think it would soften the blow if it came from you." "No problem, Eric I will take care of it."

Art and Julie had their choice of any car in the rental agency's lot. The airport and everything around it was almost totally abandoned. They loaded the overnight bags in the truck of the fire engine red mustang. Art checked his watch. The ships at Hyde Park and Victoria Park had left hours ago. He turned to Julie. We have to make a run for the Royal Family's space ship. Julie nodded in agreement. It was the closest and after all, he had recently been knighted surely they could hitch a ride with the Queen. The pebbles that fell from the sky bounced off the hood of the car like tiny marbles. As they motored down the highway, Julie had the look of worry on her face. She could hear Art mummer under his breath. "Crap. Bloody hell. Son of a…" "Art! Calm down. If you wreck the car, we will never get there." "Julie, it's dark, traffic is a nightmare and I can't see the lines in the road because of all the friggin dirt. Would you like to have a go at it?" Julie looked at him with surprise. Art had never used that tone on her before. Art tried to hide his feelings but for the first time in all the years she had known him, Art was afraid and she knew it. Julie tried to be supportive. She gently caressed the back of his neck. "Luv, she spoke in a reassuring voice. It's going to be okay." Just then, a stone hit the windshield. Pow! There was a huge crack on the right side of the window. Suddenly, it was like driving through a bad hailstorm. Windshields were cracking and breaking all over the road. Drivers and passengers abandoned their vehicles to seek shelter leaving the road littered with cars. Julie and Art had no choice but to do like wise. They grabbed their bags and headed for shelter under a large evergreen. "Look," said Julie "lights, up ahead. I think it's a rest stop." The two held their bags over their heads and made a mad dash for the rest stop. After Art caught his breath, he looked around at the frightened people who came in looking for safe haven. "We are so screwed!" He said. "Hello!" A young boy around twelve came up to Art. "Aren't you Sir Arthur Collins?" He asked. "Why yes," Art was surprised to be recognized. "Could I have your autograph?" Asked the boy. He handed Art a napkin and pen. When the kid went to rejoin his parents Art turned to Julie. "That's it! The Prime Minister once told me that if I ever needed anything to let him know." There was only one pay phone in the whole place and the line was to the door. "Try the cell, Art." Art waived the phone at Julie's face. "It doesn't work. Remember I tried calling Will and Matt at the airport." "That was to the states, she said. Just try it please. I don't want to die here." Tears welled up in Julie's eyes and her voice was cracking. Art had Prime Minister Major's number on speed dial. As the two huddled in the corner Art clutched the phone with both hands while Julie said a short prayer. "It's ringing Julie!" "Artie, keep your voice down." Two rings, three rings. By the sixth ring, Art's hopes had begun to fade when suddenly. "Hello, this is Minister Major." Art exhaled "Prime Minster why are you answering your own phone?" "I sent the staff to......wait a minute, Arthur is that you?" "Yes, sir. It's Art." "How was your flight? Are you alright?" "Well, that's why I am calling sir." I have a bit of a problem. Art explained his predicament to the Prime Minister. He instructed Art to wait behind the rest stop. "A military Hummer will pick you up stirghtaway".

It was daybreak before the Hummer arrived. It was made for off road travel. While the sergeant loaded their bags in the back he explained why he was delayed. "Sorry, it took me so long to get here, sir. I had to use these cutters to get through a few fences along the way. I will have you and the Mrs. there in a couple of hours." Art smiled and thanked the solider for coming but the storm had worsened since last night and the Queen's ship may not be there in a few hours. It was five in the morning in Washington. Everyone was aboard safely when the President gave the captain of Space Force One the order to lift off. The large ship slowly rose from the ground and began to tilt to the side. The captain was forced to abort take off. After checking and double-checking, he gave the order to lift off again, but the result was the same. Four attempts were made and four times the ship tilted to the left and began to topple over. President Eric went to the bridge. "What seems to be the problem Captain?" "Sorry sir, but the gyro, it's the stabilizer. Ah, well sir it doesn't seem to be functioning properly. It's supposed to keep the ship level. If we take off the ship will fall to its side like a spinning top, sir." Eric was furious. "I thought this ship was checked out! Take me to the engine room or wherever the hell this gyro thing is and have Mrs. Robinson meet me there."

The President had Mrs. Robinson contact Harry and Zonola aboard the Big Apple for a ship-to-ship conference. A video camera was connected so that Harry could see the problem part. "Harry, we are in a real jam here. Where is your ship?" "Hi, Mr. President we made out exit from the astral corridor about ten minutes ago and have now entered the Flash lanes. How can I help you?" President Thompson told Harry the problem. Harry had them remove the part. Harry asked the crew technician how much the part weighted. "About five pounds, sir." Harry's face turned grim. "This is bad Mr. President very, very bad. When the gyro is operating there should be colored lights flashing inside the crystal. This looks a lot like Plexiglas. A gyro for a ship that size should be at least forty pounds. I am afraid you have been had." "Sorry Harry, you are breaking up. Please repeat." Harry tried again. "Sabotaged, sir." "We are losing the signal, going out of range. May God bless you and your shipmate's sir, good…" Harry was gone. Mrs. Robinson shook her head in disbelief. "We had no way of knowing," she said. "They never replaced the gyro's on the other ships. He knew we would not find out until it was too late." Eric held the plastic in his hands. He looked down as if he were speaking to it. "Even from the grave Rotart still taunts us." Eric smashed the gyro onto the floor and stormed out of the room. "All the other ships had left the region." Mrs. Robinson turned to the four crew members and tried to manage a smile. "Well boys, it's in God's hands now." President Thompson heard Mrs. Robinson's comment as he walked down the hall.

All things considered Art, Julie and their driver were making good progress but not good enough. The Sergeant drove for three hours stopping occasionally to cut open a fence or two. The terrain was rough and there was no let up of the storm. He jumped back behind the wheel when Art and Julie's worst nightmare came true. There was a call on the walkie-talkie. "Sergeant this is Brigadier Baker. I have been instructed by the Queen to inform you that her Majesty's vessel was in danger and could not be delayed any longer. Her ship departed about ten minutes ago followed by the Prime Minister's ship. His was the last to leave. He wanted to wait but was pressured by MI6 and just about everyone else to depart straightaway. Your orders are to proceed with your passengers to bunker 55 located on The East end. Are you familiar with that Sergeant?" "Yes sir," he replied. "Well then, proceed. God speed." The Brigadier had a loud booming voice so Julie and Art heard the entire conversation. Julie grabbed her stomach as if she were about to throw up. There was no mistaking what he had said. Julie could take no more. She broke down and cried. Art held her close. "It's okay. At least we are together."

Back in the states, the President assembled his staff but no one had any ideas. Eric strolled back and forth. "How do you fight a dead man?" He asked himself. "I refuse to be defeated by a parasite like Rotart." "Mrs. Robinson use the ships public address system". He instructed her to put out a call for every Spiritual leader on the ship. Will and Matt had gotten to know Eric quite well. Eric was a fighter. He hated to lose. Will leaned over to Matt. "This should be interesting." When they arrived every Spiritual leader was given a community room to assemble the faithful. An aide approached the President. "All of the rooms are packed, sir." "Good," said Eric. "Then line them up in the halls." Sara could hear a few of the aids whispering among themselves. "It's light out we're all going to die." she heard one say. "He's just trying to keep them from looking at how bad it's gotten over night." Sara knew better. She had also gotten to know the President. Eric asked everyone in the room to hold hands while Mrs. Robinson led them in prayer. One of the aides named Anthony refused to participate.. "This is crazy," he snapped. "We are gong to die and you know it." Mrs. Robinson turned to the scared young man. "Yes, Anthony we are all going to die someday, but not today." They prayed without him. In fact, for almost an hour just about everyone on the ship even those listening over the loud speakers prayed. When it was over everyone returned to his or her room except the President's staff. Eric took Mrs. Robinson by the hand. "Thank you," he said. Anthony stood up and yelled from across the room. "Yeah! A lot of good that did we are still stranded." The room was crowded and Matt, Will and Sara were sitting on the floor. Suddenly Matt leaped to his feet. "No! We are not stranded!" He turned to his wife. "T'zar!," he said. "They are here. Yes!" He ran over to the window. Will, Sara and Eric followed. Anthony would not keep quiet. "Hey Sara," he called out, "your husband's nuts. There ain't nothing out there but dirt and rocks." Will stepped to Anthony. He stood right in his face. "I think that we have heard about enough from you. It's time for you to shut up and find a seat." Anthony could tell that Will's tone indicated that he was not just making a suggestion. He quickly took Will's advice and found a seat in the corner.

Only Will, Eric and Sara knew the special connection between Matt and T'zar. Eventually everyone came over to look but could see nothing but the rich brown dirt that had been falling for more than a day now. Then out of thin air there it was. "Look." Sara said. Just as Matt had predicted a humungous ship began to materialize right before their eyes. There was jumping, screaming, high fives, and hugs all around. A familiar voice came from the other vessel through the com system. "Mr. President, request permission to come aboard?" It was T'zar. He had come to rescue them and he was not alone.

Everyone headed out to greet T'zar. Everyone except Anthony. He now had a clear view of the rescue ship. Mrs. Walker turned to Anthony and gave him a smile and a wink. It was too much for him to handle so he simply passed out. T'zar opened the covered walkway that extended between the two vessels. As he crossed, Matt noticed that Onan, Lysta and Nyssa were close behind. "I bid you peace. It is good to see you again my friends." T'zar had a big grin on his face. The others were smiling too. "I bid you peace." said T''zar. "The planet Teldran is rapidly approaching." "We haven't much time," said Onan. "We were able to monitor your transmission to the Big Apple ship, but the Centurion War Ships delayed our arrival. If we had attempted to make contact, our presence would have been discovered. We concealed our ship by hiding on the far side of your moon as a precaution in case the cloak failed. We came as soon as the last Centurion left. We got here as quickly as we could." Will had lots of questions but the answers would have to wait. "How did you know we would need your help? Where did you get that ship?" T'zar laughed. Matt thought it was odd seeing T'zar so loose and relaxed. He always seemed so serious. "Will my friend," T'zar patted Will on the back. "Let's just say we liberated it from the government. This is the prototype to the ships you have been building. It was deicded that because Earth took so long to respond to the circles this ship would be too difficult for your pilots to master in such a short period of time. It's larger, faster and has more power. We heard that Rotart duped many of your countries leaving millons stranded that is why we have returned." "Sorry to interrupt. I am Eric Thompson President of the United States. I hate to be so forward, but is it possible that we could install your gyro system into our ship?" Nyssa stepped forward and shook Eric's hand. "It's an honor to finally meet you Mr. President. I am sorry but that will not be possible. Our gyro is much too large for your ship. It would be wise for you to begin evacuating your ship immediatly. We will open decks A through J. We must act quickly. The planet draws closer with each passing moment." Eric was qiuick to take control of the transfer. "Yes," he said to one of the aides, "people, food, personal belongs, everything that's not nailed down." The President leaned forward to speak into the ships communication system. "Ladies and Gentlemen, we have been rescued." Thunderous cheers and applause rang out throughout Space Force 1. Will turned to Onan. "That was one hell of an entrance." he said. Onan pointed to Nyssa. "The cloaking device was Nyssa's idea. She installed it on the way. We were able to avoid the patrol ship but the Lazon warships would have surely detected us as soon as we de-cloaked outside your ship." Nyssa looked around the room. "Where is Arthur?" She asked Matt shrugged his shoulders. "Not sure. We hope he got out on one of the other ships but he may still be in London." "What? Why haven't you contacted him? Will lend me your communication device." Will was clearly caught off guard. "Ah, well, um. I left it back in my room." Matt reached into his back pocket. "No problem use mine." He handed it to T'zar. After a bit of tweaking T'zar pushed the gray button near the bottom.

Art, Julie, and Sarge were nearing the bunker when the device in his overnight bag started to beep. "Sarge, stop the car!" It took sometime for Art to figure out how to communicate using the device. T'zar instructed him to go to Stonehenge. "Why are we going there?" Asked Julie. "You may not believe this but we are going to be rescued. Matt and Will never got off the planet. Their ship was sabotaged. Another ship just came to transfer everything to the new ship; it may take a few hours from the looks of things we don't' have that long." Sarge interrupted the conversation. "Excuse me, sir." This windshield is made of bulletproof glass but these pebbles are turning into stones. "I am not sure if we can make it." Julie was still confused. She tapped Art on the shoulder to finish her conversation. "Artie, tell me again why are we going to Stonehenge. Is there a ship there?" "No." said Art. "Well I don't think so. You see there are a few things that I haven't told you. You see, apparently there is something there that can help us." Once again, Art is interrupted by Sarge. "Sir, things are looking up. The back roads are clear. If we can maintain this speed, we will be there in no time."

Matt, Will and the Lazonians decided to table their discussion until after the ship was loaded. It was a massive effort. Everyone could see that the sky had turned completely brown, and even if you didn't look up you could hear the relentless pinging of the pebbles and dirt hitting both ships. The passengers and crew moved at a frantic pace. Even the children pitched in. People were running back and forth across the covered ramps carrying furniture, food, supplies and everything else in site. Onan stopped briefly to look at the sky. "It is going to be close." he said. Nyssa and Lysta monitored communications in the control room. They were expecting Art to call at any minute. Sarge pulled up the hummer close to the structure at Stonehenge. "I can't believe we made it. We are almost out of petro." There was a group of people chanting under a make shift tent near the circle. Art dialed Nyssa, once he got through Lysta called T'zar and Onan back to the control room. T'zar took over. "Art I need you and Julie to run to the center of the henge." Art was reluctant to leave the Sarge behind. "Come on man. You can't stay here. Where are we going?" Asked the Sarge. "There he pointed. There's no ship, nobody to pick us up." "Just trust me," he said. T'zar spoke into the mike. "Art turn your communicator over and slide the back off. The green button is the antenna, push it." Art watched as the antenna shot up. The storm was getting worse. Sarge took off his coat to shield the three of them. "Okay, what's next?" he asked. "Press the blue button three times them press the numbers 5972, and then press the red button once. Hold the device high over your head and what ever happens do not lower your arm." "Okay. I will give it a go." said Art. He did as T'zar instructed him and asked Sarge to remove the coat. Nothing happened.

Nyssa tapped T'zar on the back. "I think you should take a look at this." She pointed to a screen that she was monitoring. "The blue dot is Art. I don't' know what the red dot is. I can only tell you that it is metallic and it's rapidly aprocahing Art's position." T'zar turned back to the speaker. "Art you must hurry. Walk from one end of the circle counting each step. When you reach the other side divide the number by two. Use that number to find the exact number of steps to the center. Hurry!" "Getting closer." yelled Nyssa. Lysta peered into the screen. "Oh no, I know what it is." she cried. "It's the Space Station." Again, Art raised his arm high. Julie and Sarge stood close by. Pebbles, dust, stones, and now rocks were hailing down on them. Suddenly cobalt blue lighting flashes and white sparks started to shoot out of the communication device. The loud popping and crackling noises rang out overhead. It was difficult but Art held on with both hands. Several of the chanters saw what was going on and started to run towards them. Julie tried to wave them off but they just kept coming. There was a loud crackle and in a instant the center of the henge was clear. A millisecond later they re-appeared in a somewhat calmer environment. Art, Julie, Sarge and a half dozen uninvited guests were transported thousands of miles. "Bloody hell! Where are we?" said Sarge. A mere eight seconds later, the Universal Space Station came crashing down to Earth with such force that it destroyed Stonehenge the Hummer and everything around it. The ground shook so violently from the impact of the flaming twisted white hot metal. That what use to be Stonehenge was now a massive crater filled with smoldering embers and red hot rocks. "Art, its Nyssa. You are in Stonehenge, New Hampshire. The weather is not as severe over here. Not yet anyway. We needed to buy you some time." "Thanks Nyssa but it's getting pretty rough here too. How soon can you pick us up? We are still getting hammered here." Nyssa turned to Onan. "We need at least another forty-five minutes."

Eric and Matt walked in on the call. "President Thompson we have transported Art to New Hampshire but we do not have the technology to bring them here. They will not last much longer in this storm. We have a dilemma." Onan handed the communication device to Eric. "Art, this is Eric. How long do you think you can hang on?" "Hell, Mr. President. We are pretty banged up. Fifteen maybe twenty minutes tops." Eric looked around the room. "Any suggestions?" Lysta looked at Nyssa. "The Silver Unicorn!" Eric squinted his eyes in a look of confusion. "The Silver what?" "It is our ship. It is in the cargo hole." explained Lysta. "It will give them shelter until you come for us. Nyssa, let's go!" By the time Lysta and Nyssa landed the Unicorn the stones falling from the sky had had turned to small rocks. Julie, Art and Sarge had to be helped board. A few new comers also sought refuge inside the small ship. All total the Silver Unicorn packed in fourteen passengers. The ship was taking a pounding from the barrage of stone and rocks. Communication with Space Force was down. "Nyssa we cannot take much more of this." "Lysta, I know. I have an idea."

The new Space Force One was almost completely loaded when Sara looked out of the window to see about two hundred people banging on the entrance doors to the ship. She turned to T'zar. "How many people did you say this ship could hold?" "51,000." he replied. "Thanks." she said as she ran out of the room and raced to the massive ships doors entrance. She struggled to pull the red latch open. When the doors finally slid open, the batter and bruised people came pouring in. Some grabbed her and hugged her while others collapsed on the floor. "Bless you, oh God bless you." "Thanks." They all wanted to show their gratitude. It seems that at the last minute they had a change of heart about staying. Sara was not done. She sized up the last man as he came in and said. "Give me your coat." The man looked puzzled, but he compiled with her request. Sara held the heavy winter coat over her head as she dashed across the dirt-covered lawn to the abandoned ship tripping on stones and rocks along the way. The door was partially opened. She picked up a board and managed to pry the door open enough to squeeze inside. Once inside she opened the doors using the automated panel. By the time Sara returned to Space Force One sweat was pouring off of her as if she had just stepped out of a sauna. "I have been looking all over for you" said Matt. "What the heck were you doing out there?" Sara was out of breath, she could hardly speak but she managed to get out a few words. "Stragglers," she said. "More people coming after we leave. Need to give them shelter."

Matt informed her that they were finally ready for take-off but the Silver Unicorn was missing. "We can't communicate with them and there's no sign of them on radar. We can't even reach Art. Onan thinks his communication was damaged by the storm." Onan and T'zar were at the controls. The smoldering rocks were getting larger, not to mention the occasional Volkswagen size boulders. All of the ships entrances was sealed and the new Space Force One was finally air born. As they lifted off a boulder the size of a mini van crashed directly into the White House. A glimpse out of the window showed small fires burning on Pennsylvania Avenue and all over downtown D.C. From Sara's vantage point she could see a dozen or so people headed toward the abandoned ship. She pressed her hand against the window and smiled. By the time the ship reached New Hampshire it was raining fire.

Onan turned to T'zar. "No sign of the Unicorn. They must be around here somewhere. They could not have abandoned ship. It's close to 100 degrees out there." Eric asked T'zar to look for wreckage among the trees. "Wreckage," T'zar repeated. "Nyssa can out fly anyone on the planet. Even on her bad days. No, Mr. President believe me they are close by. Onan take us to that body of water over there and level off at an altitude of 200 feet." "Alright," good idea T'zar. "If we are in plain sight, we will be easier to spot." Rocks, stones, dirt and more than a few boulders rained down around them. You could hear and feel the impact as they bounced off the ships hull. Matt was getting nervous again. Before he could open his mouth T'zar turned to him and said "Do not worry my friend. She is a strong vessel you are safe, for now." Matt looked East then West then East again. T'zar turned to Matt once again. "What is it Matt?" "Well T'zar, how come the sky is brown in the West and blue in the East?" Everyone turned from the monitors to look out of the large windows to see what all the fuss was about. Will's jaw suddenly dropped "Oh my God. There is no horizon. That's not the sky," he said. He paused for a moment and stared out the window. "It's the ocean. It's the Tsunami!" The wall of water rushing toward them was so high that it blocked out the entire sky. What was left of the planet Teldran had begun to impact the ocean. Eric rushed over to Tzar. "You gotta get us out of here!" "We have time," said T'zar in a calm voice."It is still a ways off. Onan, how far away are we?" "1,200 feet and closing fast," he said. The room was still, not another word was spoken everyone was searching the skies for Silver Unicorn while keeping an eye on the rapidly approaching wall of water. "There! Over there!" Matt pointed downward into the sea. "Something shiny just moved." Moments later the Silver Unicorn gracefully sliced through the ocean's surface and went airborne traveling at a high rate of speed away from the ship. "Open the bay doors!" Shouted T'zar. "She's coming in." Nyssa maneuvered the Unicorn in a sweeping U-turn and headed for the open bay doors. She banked left and glided the battered ship straight into the hanger. With the Unicorn safely on board every ones attention to turn to the Tsunami. "One hundred and twenty two feet." cried Onan.

T'zar pointed to Onan. "Go!" Everyone on the ships bridge breathed a sigh of relief, but no one was more relieved than Eric. The wait from years of planning and setbacks from Rotart was finally over. They were on their way to the New Earth. Matt, Will, Mrs. Robinson, Art, Sara, Julie, Eric, T'zar, Onan, Lysta, Nyssa, and Sarge held a brief reunion and celebration on the ship's bridge. Someone open a bottle of Champagne and Eric proposed a toast to lasting friendships old and new on Earth 2. Onan called T'zar over to the controls. Matt caught the two whispering. "What's up guys?" Asked Matt. Onan pointed to a flashing purple symbol on one of the ship's control panel. "It is the cloaking for the ship. One of the rocks must have damaged it. We used it to pass by the Lazorian's centurions, at the gate on the way in. They would have recognized this as the missing ship. I am sure that its disappearance has been reported to them. We do not want to run into them on the way to the New Planet." Matt put his arm around on Onan's shoulder and looked him in the eye. "So what you told me was true. You guys really did rip this ship off?" He laughed. "Unbelievable, so how do we get to the gate?" "Vada," said Lysta. "We use the gate at Vada." She looked at Matt. "Ok if you still want to call it Mars that's fine with me. It is not that far away and this ship is much faster than the others. I am certain that we will be the first to land on the new planet." "Wait a second." Matt put down the glass of champagne, and used his hands to form a pyramid. "I thought that each gate or portal was marked by a pyramid. There are no pyramids on Mars so how could there be a portal?" Nyssa gently pulled Matt's hands apart. "Matt, one thing you will learn is that in time every planet reclaims what is hers. Every pyramid is constructed from the soil and in time will be reclaimed by it. Such has been the case of Mars. Trust us. The pyramid may be gone but the portal remains."

"May I have your attention please?" The President interrupted the group's conversations. "Tonight I am holding a real celebration to honor all of you who have made this possible. I will see you all at 10:00." The chefs of Space Force One did a great job of planning the party especially with such short notice. Everyone from the Lazonians to the President's Cabinet was in attendance there. The food was plentiful and there was lots of singing and laughter. Eric, Will, Onan, T'zar and Art were sitting around the table drinking and reliving the eight year odyssey. Will had been waiting all day to hear the Lazonians story about how they happened to return to Earth with the replacement ship.

"Yo T'zar, how did you guys pull this off? Won't you be missed by your people? What happed to all the secrecy? I am afraid not my friend. Maybe our friends will miss us but not our rulers. We won't be returning to Lazon. Onan and I have been banished." "What!" said Eric. "You mean you were caught helping us?" "Not exactly."

Onan explained. "Some time ago the government impounded and searched our ship but did not find anything, obviously they were tipped off. Then again two months ago, our ship was seized again but this time the interior taken apart. We were given a trial and convicted of unlawful travel to a restricted planet. Yours." T'zar reached into his shirt pocket and pulled out a small plastic bag. "I keep this as a memento," he said. He dumped the contents onto the table. It was a small ball of foil and a tiny strip of paper with the word Hershey written on it. Will examined it and put it back on the table. "I don't get it." He said to T'zar dumbfounded. "It's just a candy wrapper. What's the big deal?" T'zar put the wrapper back into the bag. "This was found wedged in the seat cushion on our ship. No such treats exists on our world. It was not enough to prove that we were in League with your governments but the evidence was sufficient for the government to place us in exile. I guess you can say that we are now homeless." "Not if I can help it." President Thompson spoke up. "In the eyes of all Americans, you people are heroes. You have a home on Earth 2 for as long as you and your people want to stay. I insist." "Thank You. Mr. President, you are most generous. We cannot take credit for liberating this vessel our brothers and sisters, borrowed it from the government. They said it was a going away present from Earth's Guardians. Who would have thought that something as small as a candy wrapper would end up saving thousands of people?" Matt and Sara came over to the table to say goodnight.

Sara was on cloud nine. On the way to their quarters she told Matt how she felt about what she experienced today. "You know Matt, all these years I walked around feeling sorry for myself after we lost the baby, but today, today I started looking at life differently. I actually helped people. You should have seen their faces. As we were flying over the White House, I looked down and saw dozens of people running toward the ship we left behind for shelter. Starting today, I am going to appreciate life more." she kissed Matt in the elevator. By the time they reached the room Sara was feeling frisky.

Several months later. The ships doctor confirmed that Sara was indeed pregnant again. The journey to Earth Two was long but productive. There was plenty of food, entertainment and recreation but most of all there was a great exchange of cultures from around the world. Barriers were broken down and many lasting friendships were formed. President Thompson held ship-to-ship conferences with world leaders on a daily bases. They was much to be done an entire world needed to be constructed. At last, the day had come when New Earth appeared outside the windows of the ship. Everyone rushed to get a glimpse of their new home. Everyone except Sara that is, she was in labor. Two minutes after the ship touched down Sara delivered a healthy baby girl. To every ones surprise, three minutes after the girl was delivered Sara had a baby boy. The twins were the first children to be born on the New Planet. President Eric Thompson was the first human to set foot on the pristine planet. It was beautiful. He carried the American flag with him. Eric walked a few feet away from the ship and jammed the flagpole in to the Earth. "On behalf of the United States government and it's citizens, I claim this land as Earth Two for the New United States of America."

Everyone cheered and raced out of the ship like school kids at recess. Some kissed the ground a few just stood and cried. Shortly after their arrival the sky was filled with the rest of the fleet arriving from Earth. Will and Art joined Matt in the delivery room. They watched the proceedings from the window. Will kissed Sara on the forehead, and shook hands with Matt and Art. "Well guys we did it. We have been given a second chance. Let's hope this time we get it right."

Book #2

Return 2 Earth

It's been eight years since the nearly six billion people have been evacuated from Earth. The Millions left behind were forced into slavery by the heartless dictator Taz. Earth is slowly drifting toward the Sun and the rescue mission by New Earth has been hampered by a clever spy. Matt, Will, and Art must travel the galaxies in search of ancient symbols and clues in order to build a super weapon capable of destroying Taz's armada of warships and army. Along the way they encounter new alien species like the tree dwellers of the Indigo forest on the planet Tygalon. The trio travel to Lazon to link up once again with Earth's Guardians. Deadly plants, the lighting fast warships of the Scorpion fleet, and advanced alien technologies such as Trans-matts are the norm for this adventure. The ruthless Taz has marked our heroes for death. Will the spy be caught in time? Can the humans outwit the crafty Taz and rescue the millions of men women and children left to perish as the rays of the Sun turns what's left of Earth into a ragging inferno or will Taz make good on his promise to kill Will, Matt, and Art? Will they Return 2 Earth in time?

978-0-595-38935-
0-595-38935-X

Printed in the United Kingdom by
Lightning Source UK Ltd., Milton Keynes
138265UK00002B/192/A